MR. MIDNIGHT

Gordan Cross, crime reporter for the *Daily Clarion*, is detailed to discover the identity of a man known as Mr. Midnight, the mastermind behind a series of robberies and murders. Acting on a tip, he investigates The Yellow Orchid nightclub — and meets a variety of odd and suspicious people, including two who quickly turn up dead. How is the classy club implicated in the Midnight business — and who is the mysterious informant, 'A. Smith'? Teamed with Superintendent Budd of Scotland Yard, Gordan is determined to uncover the truth.

GERALD VERNER

◆

MR. MIDNIGHT

Complete and Unabridged

LINFORD
Leicester

First published in Great Britain

First Linford Edition
published 2019

A catalogue record for this book is available
from the British Library.

ISBN 978–1–4448–4050–6

Published by
F. A. Thorpe (Publishing)
Anstey, Leicestershire

Set by Words & Graphics Ltd.
Anstey, Leicestershire
Printed and bound in Great Britain by
T. J. International Ltd., Padstow, Cornwall

This book is printed on acid-free paper

Prologue

It was raining: thin grey curtains of rain that swept before an east wind. Along the Great North Road, the headlights of a lorry shone blearily through the wet darkness, glistening on the green of hedges and lighting up the streaming blackness of the macadamized surface.

Bert Wilson peered through the windscreen at the road ahead with tired red-rimmed eyes. He had been driving all night, and the lightening of the sky in the east told him that it was nearly dawn. He had left Nottingham at seven o'clock the previous evening, but engine trouble, followed by a flat tyre, had delayed him.

It had been his unlucky night, he thought as he steered the heavy lorry round a bend. Never mind, it was nearly over. A mile or so further on, there was a little wayside cafe that catered for lorry drivers. He could pull up there for a cup of coffee and some cigarettes, and then

1

do the comparatively short run to London.

The dim lights of the low-roofed little shack came in sight a few minutes later. There were two other lorries drawn up outside the place, and Bert pulled his in behind the rearmost. Opening the door, he climbed stiffly down from his cab, crossed the strip of rough grass before the cafe, and entered.

The lights were not very bright, but they dazzled him after the long period of darkness outside. Two or three men were standing at the counter, smoking and drinking thick mugs of coffee. Behind the counter, in a soiled white coat, the bartender was cutting a sandwich.

Bert ordered a coffee. 'With sugar, mate,' he said, 'an' make it snappy.'

A man who had his back to him turned at the sound of his voice. ''Lo, Bert,' he greeted. 'Late, ain't yer?'

'A bit,' said Bert, rubbing his cold hands. ''Ad engine trouble an' a burst. Blimey, what a night, ain't it? The rain's like a perishin' curtain. You can't see more'n a few feet in front of yer 'eadlights.'

'Don't look like stoppin' neither.

2

Wot'cher carryin'?'

'Load o' fags, Tom,' answered Bert. He grinned. 'an' I been gaspin' fer a smoke. Funny, ain't it? 'Urry up with that perishin' cawfee, will yer? an' give us a packet o' Woods.'

'Ten or twenty?' asked the barman.

'Twenty.'

The barman flipped a twenty packet of Woodbines towards him.

'Thanks, mate,' said Bert. He lit one, inhaled the smoke deeply, and let it trickle slowly through his nostrils. 'Ah,' he breathed, 'that's better. Wanted that, I did. 'Ow's the missus, Tom?'

Tom shook his head. 'Poorly, mate. She ain't never really got over young Ted, yer know. Don't say much, but yer can see she's broodin' over it.'

The barman pushed a steaming mug across the counter. ''Ere's yer cawfee,' he said tersely.

Bert threw him a crumpled ten-shilling note. He picked up the mug and gulped at the scalding liquid it contained. 'Pity you 'as ter leave 'er so much on 'er own, Tom. If you could . . . '

The sound of an engine starting up outside stopped him and brought his head up with a jerk.

'Blimey, that's the old bus!' he exclaimed. ''Ere, what's 'appenin'?'

He banged the mug of coffee down on the counter, slopping it over, and ran to the door. Tom and the other two men followed him. As they peered out into the rain, the engine revved faster. Bert ran across the rough grass strip towards the place where he had parked his lorry. Dimly he could see a man behind the wheel and another just climbing into the cab.

''Ere,' he shouted, 'wot'cher doin' with that lorry, eh? Come on out of it!'

The man who was climbing in turned. 'You get away,' he snarled. 'Keep out of it or you'll get hurt, see.'

'Tryin' a pinch, eh?' cried Bert. 'Well, you can perishin' well come on out of it!' He made a grab at the door of the cab.

'You fool,' cried the man. 'Let go o' that door . . . let go, do you hear?' He brought his closed fist down on Bert's fingers.

'I'll see yer in 'ell first,' retorted Bert. 'Just you come on out of it!'

He shifted his hold and gripped the other's wrist. The man tried to shake him off, but he clung on desperately. The lorry began to move.

'Let go, will you?' snarled the man, trying to wrench himself free.

'Don't argue — let him have it,' growled the man at the wheel.

'All right, you've asked for it,' said the other. Something exploded almost in Bert's face. An agonizing pain shot through his head, and as the lorry gathered speed, he fell back onto the wet road.

'Bert . . . Bert!' Tom, running up, nearly fell over him. 'Are you 'urt, mate?'

But there was no answer from the sprawling figure at his feet. A man cannot speak with a bullet in his brain, and Bert had died before his body touched the road on which he lay.

1

John Tully, the news editor of the *Daily Clarion*, threw a bunch of flimsies down on his desk and looked up at Dowling, the chief sub.

'I've never known such an epidemic of robbery and violence, Dowling,' he grunted. 'It's the result of this shortage of everything, of course. There's an easy sale for stolen stuff in the black market these days, and the wide boys are taking full advantage of it.'

Dowling nodded. 'There's a new and dangerous element crept in, Mr. Tully,' he said. 'These fellows never used to carry firearms.'

'That's what's making it serious. Look at that poor devil of a lorry driver last week. Shot down in cold blood!'

'And the watchman at that warehouse.'

'You could go on quoting instances all night,' growled Tully.

'Cross has an idea that these robberies

and murders aren't isolated cases,' said the chief sub. 'He thinks they're being organized.'

John Tully looked suddenly interested. 'By somebody working the black market on a colossal scale? Hm, now there might be something in that. Where's Cross?'

'In the reporters' room.'

'Go and ask him to come here, will you?'

Dowling picked up the wad of flimsies and hurried away. Tully removed his horn-rimmed glasses and rubbed his eyes. A boy staggering with a tray of tea came by and put a cup on the desk. The news editor was gulping it down when Gordan Cross appeared.

'You want me?' he asked cheerfully.

'Yes — Dowling says you think this crime wave isn't the work of separate gangs,' said Tully. 'Is that right?'

'Not altogether,' answered Cross. 'What I believe is that all the stolen stuff goes to one central depot.'

'A kind of super-fence, eh?'

'Something of the sort.'

'Is this just a theory of yours, Cross? Or

have you any concrete reason?'

'I've no actual evidence,' admitted the crime reporter, 'but I've heard several rumours. There's definitely somebody at the back of all these robberies . . . somebody who's buying the stolen stuff in a big way, and for good prices.'

'Any idea who it is?'

'No, but I've heard hints and whispers among the wide boys that there is such a person.'

'Find him, Cross,' said Tully curtly. 'That's your job from now on. I want the full story — with the identity of this mysterious person, if he exists.'

'He exists, Mr. Tully, I'm sure of that. Whether I can find him is another matter.'

John Tully put on his glasses. The look he gave his chief crime reporter was what the office usually referred to as 'formidable'.

'You're the crime man on this paper, aren't you?' he said. 'All right! If you want to remain so, you'll get that story!'

★　★　★

The Blue Feathers was an unsalubrious public house sited on the corner of a side turning in Deptford Broadway. The outside lacked paint, and what paint was there was hidden under years of sooty grime. Inside, the bars remained as they were at the time when Queen Victoria was a girl. The red plush of seats and hangings had faded and blackened, the mirrors had developed black spots and streaks; some were cracked, the gilt and plaster of their elaborate frames had fallen away, and the whole place bore the stamp of decayed grandeur.

The frequenters of The Blue Feathers were, mercifully, not concerned with the artistic elegance of their surroundings. The beer was good, and that was all that troubled them. For the most part, the public house was better than the slums in which they lived, and anyway, they were not discriminating. For here came nightly all the worst element of Deptford to forget their troubles or celebrate some bit of luck.

A thin fog hung clammily over that squalid neighbourhood as Gordan Cross came briskly along the Broadway Road and turned into the saloon bar of The Blue Feathers. It had come up from the river with nightfall, thin and tenuous at first, but rapidly thickening. Before morning, unless the rain came and washed it away, it looked like developing into a real pea-souper.

The bar was fairly full, and Gordan paused just inside the door, searching for the man he had come to find. He saw him after a moment or two, standing by the bar. He was a little man with thin nondescript features and narrow, stooping shoulders. His overcoat was shabby and a size too big for his meagre frame. Cross made his way towards him.

''Nother pint o' mild an' bitter, Charley,' the piping voice of the little man reached his ears as he drew near. 'an' don't go makin' it nearly all mild this time.'

'Don't know what yer talkin' about,' said the barman. 'If yer asks fer mild an' bitter, yer gets mild an' bitter 'ere, see?'

'That last one I 'ad ruddy well wasn't.'

The barman's battered face darkened.

'Now look 'ere, Williams. I don't want none o' your lip.'

'Have this one with me and don't argue, Nosey,' said Gordan.

Nosey Williams swung round. There was a startled look in his small eyes which faded as he recognized the reporter. ''Ullo, Mr. Cross,' he said. 'I didn't know you was 'ere.'

'I've only just come in,' said Gordan. He lowered his voice. 'Get your drink and come away from the bar, Nosey. I want to talk to you.'

'I wish you wouldn't call me Nosey,' whispered the little informer, glancing uneasily over his shoulder. 'If some o' the boys was to 'ear yer . . . '

'Everybody calls you Nosey,' said Cross calmly. 'If you think it isn't known that you supply information to the police now and again, you're kidding yourself. Two mild and bitters, please.' This last aloud to the barman.

'Nobody ain't never been able ter prove nothing,' muttered Nosey. 'Wot'cher want ter see me about?'

'Bring your beer over to that corner

and I'll tell you,' said Gordan. He nodded to a corner of the bar that was deserted.

Nosey Williams's face wrinkled into a worried expression, but he said nothing. When the beer arrived and Gordan had paid for it, he handed one glass to his companion and picked up the other. 'Come on, over here,' he said.

Nosey followed him reluctantly. When they reached the corner, he looked up at the reporter. 'Well, wot'cher want?' he asked.

Gordan assured himself that there was nobody near enough to overhear him before he replied. 'Remember what you were telling me the other night?' he said in a low voice. 'About there being somebody at the back of all these robberies — somebody high up?'

The vague uneasiness on Nosey Williams's face changed to a look of open alarm. 'I don't know what yer talking about,' he declared. 'I never said nothin' of the sort!'

'Come now, Nosey, don't try that stuff with me. I know what you said, and you know too.'

'I must've been drunk.' said the little man. His eyes were darting uneasily round the bar. 'That's it, Mr. Cross; you don't want ter take no notice o' what I said. I was tight!'

'Oh no you weren't,' said Gordan calmly. 'You'd had one or two, but you weren't drunk. Come across, Nosey — what do you know?'

'Nuthin'.' Nosey was getting more and more alarmed with every second. 'I don't know nuthin'. I never said I knew anythin'. That's the truth!'

'You wouldn't recognize the truth if it came and bit you. Come on, tell me what you know.'

'I tell yer I don't know nuthin'.'

'I'll make it worth your while.'

'Money ain't no use to a dead man,' muttered Nosey.

'So that's it, eh?' said Gordan quickly. 'You *do* know something, but you're scared. Who are you scared of?'

'Nobody. I ain't scared of nobody. Look 'ere, Mr. Cross, leave me alone, can't yer? I don't know nuthin' about what yer talkin' about. I don't — honest.'

14

'Lew Steiner was released from prison last week,' remarked Gordan conversationally. 'He's very anxious to find the man who shopped him. Shall I tell him who it was?'

The little man's face whitened. There was panic in his eyes. 'You wouldn't do that, Mr. Cross,' he whispered huskily. 'Lew 'ud kill me if he knew!'

'Then tell me what I want to know,' snapped Gordan.

Nosey Williams licked his lips. 'For Gawd's sake, Mr. Cross.'

'Who's behind this racket? You've got some idea.'

'Some feller they call . . . Mr. Midnight,' said Nosey almost inaudibly. 'That's all I know, I swear it is!'

'Mr. Midnight?' repeated Gordan.

Williams clutched his arm frantically. 'Sh-s-s-s!' he entreated fearfully. 'For Gawd's sake, don't talk so loud!'

'It's all right; there's nobody near enough to hear. Why is he called Mr. Midnight?'

''Cos that's the time 'e always meets 'em ter pay off fer a job,' whispered

Nosey. 'Don't ask me any more, Mr. Cross.'

'Where?' persisted Gordan. 'Where does this meeting take place?'

'I dunno — different places.' Nosey gulped some beer. 'Look 'ere, Mr. Cross, I don't want ter get mixed up in it.'

'Rather get mixed up with Steiner, eh, Nosey?' asked Gordan pleasantly.

'It ain't fair,' whined the little man. 'It's blackmail, that's what it is!'

'It must be a change for you to be blackmailed. It's usually the other way round, isn't it? Who's this man they call Mr. Midnight?'

The door to the street opened and a man came in. He was elderly, tall, well dressed and distinguished-looking. In any gathering he would have been noticeable; among the frequenters of The Blue Feathers he stood out like a tree in the desert. At sight of him, Nosey went the colour of chalk.

'What's the matter?' asked Gordan. 'You look as if you've seen a ghost.'

'Nuthin' . . . there ain't nuthin' the matter.' Nosey's voice was almost a

16

whimper. 'Let's get out of 'ere, Mr. Cross!'

Out of the corner of his eye, Gordan saw the newcomer go over to the bar. 'Who's the man who's just come in?' he asked.

'Which man?' Nosey's voice was elaborately unconcerned. ''Im? 'Ow should I know? Look 'ere, Mr. Cross, I got ter go.' He put down his beer, half finished, and went shuffling hastily to the door.

Gordan followed him, but he was moving so quickly that he was several yards down the fog-bound street before he caught up with him. 'Not so fast,' he said. 'You *did* know that man who came in, Nosey. That's why you left so quickly. You were scared.'

'Scared? I don't know what yer talkin' about,' muttered Nosey Williams, walking so fast that Gordan found it difficult to keep up with him. 'I ain't seen that bloke before in me life.'

'He wasn't Mr. Midnight, by any chance?' asked Gordan.

'Don't I keep tellin' yer?' said Nosey. 'I don't know who 'e is. Nobody knows.'

'But you know *something*. Come on, Nosey, I'm losing patience!'

Williams stopped. It was dark here, and the thickening fog swirled round them like a blanket.

'Listen, Mr. Cross,' said the little man earnestly. 'I want ter 'elp yer. I'd like ter 'elp yer, if it don't get me inter no trouble, see. You 'eard o' The Yellow Orchid?'

'Do you mean the new roadhouse near St. Albans?' asked the reporter.

'That's the place. Ever been there?'

'No, I haven't.'

'I'd go if I was you.'

'Do you think I might find Mr. Midnight there?'

'I don't know what you'll find. I ain't sayin' nuthin' more. But I'd go, if I was you, see?'

Nosey Williams suddenly darted away across the road and was lost in the fog. Gordan stared after him for a moment, and then he began to make his way through the murk towards the station.

He felt that the evening had not been wasted.

2

Vicky Cross, looking very charming in a new gown of white satin that formed a perfect contrast to her raven hair, regarded the appointments of The Yellow Orchid with approval. The horseshoe-shaped dance floor was surrounded by a broad strip of thick-piled lilac-coloured carpet on which were set numerous tables with pale green linen cloths, each containing a cut-glass vase filled with orchids of a daffodil yellow. The chairs were upholstered in silk damask of the same daffodil hue, and the walls and ceiling were painted in yellow, trimmed with a fringe of the same lilac colour as the carpet, masking the wall-brackets, and repeated in a larger form on the centre chandelier.

'How did you find this place, Gordan?' she asked, looking across the table at her husband. 'It's lovely.'

He smiled. 'Not bad, is it?' he remarked

19

complacently. 'Jolly good band, too.'

'Yes, who is it?' said Vicky. 'Does it say on the menu?'

He picked it up and looked at it. ' 'Laddie Castell and his music',' he said after a pause. 'Hm, that's a new one on me.'

'And me,' she said. 'I don't think this place can have been open very long. It all looks so *new*.'

'It hasn't — about six months, I believe. What about another drink, darling?' He signalled to a passing waiter.

'Yes, sir?' The man came at once, waiting deferentially for the order.

'A gin and orange, Booth's if possible, with a little soda and ice, and a double whisky and ginger ale,' said Gordan.

'Yes, sir.' The waiter bowed and hurried away.

'They must be doing very well,' remarked Vicky, looking round at the crowded tables and the couples on the dance floor. 'There're a good many people here . . . Who are you staring at, Gordan?'

'That man who's just come. The tall, distinguished-looking man.'

'With grey hair, talking to the attractive

blonde?' she asked, and when he nodded: 'Do you know him?'

'No . . . no, I don't know him,' he said absently.

She looked at him suspiciously. 'Then why are you so interested?' she demanded. 'Or is the blonde the attraction?'

'No, it's not the blonde, Vicky.' He spoke without removing his eyes from the man. The suspicion in her eyes deepened.

'Gordan Cross,' she said suddenly, 'why did you suggest coming here tonight?'

'Why?' he repeated. He dragged his eyes away from the object of his interest and regarded her uneasily. 'Well, I — I thought you'd like it. We haven't been anywhere for a long time, and so . . . '

'Pish!' she said. 'That's not the real reason. I know you too well, Gordan. When you get embarrassed, you're trying to hide something. I suppose this little outing is going to figure in your expense-sheet for the *Clarion*. What are we really here for?'

He grinned sheepishly. 'Well, darling, I certainly thought of trying it,' he admitted, 'but whether they'll pass it is another matter.'

'I knew it,' she declared. 'Whenever we go anywhere, it's on some business for that wretched newspaper!'

'There's no harm in combining business with pleasure,' he protested.

Before he had time to reply, the waiter arrived with the drinks. As he was setting them down on the table, Gordan said: 'Waiter, who's that gentleman over there?'

The man followed the direction of his eyes. 'The gentleman talking to Miss Destry, sir?' he asked.

'If Miss Destry is the fair lady in blue.'

'That's Sir Franklin Marsh. He owns this place, sir.'

'Thank you.' Gordan waited until the man was out of earshot, and then he repeated softly: 'Sir Franklin Marsh? That's interesting — very interesting.'

'Is it?' asked Vicky curiously. 'Why?'

'Because that's the man who came into The Blue Feathers last night and scared Nosey Williams. Remember me telling you?'

'Gordan,' she breathed excitedly, 'is *that* why we're here? The Midnight business?'

He nodded.

'Why didn't you tell me?' she went on quickly. 'You know I'm interested in *that*. I suppose you thought if you pretended it was just a pleasure trip, I'd be more impressed?'

'Well, yes, darling,' he confessed, 'something of the sort.'

'You might have known that I should find out. Do you think Sir Franklin Marsh is the man behind all these robberies and murders?'

'I don't know. Nosey Williams was scared when he saw him in that pub, and it was Nosey who told me about this place.'

Before she could say any more, there was a long drum-roll and a clash of cymbals. The leader of the band, presumably Laddie Castell, a dark good-looking man, advanced to the front of the dais.

'Ladies and gentlemen,' he said, speaking into a microphone in a rather pleasant voice, 'we're going to play for you a new number entitled 'Send No Regrets'. The singer is Rodney Mayne.'

There was a little round of applause as he bowed and faced the band, the lights went down, and as the band began to play the introduction, a spotlight focused on the microphone. A fair-haired man came forward and began to sing in a slightly husky but very attractive voice.

'He's got quite a good voice,' remarked Gordan.

'Uh-uh.' Vicky nodded her dark head. 'Nice-looking, too.'

The number was slow, seductive, and all about a broken love affair, which seemed to be the most popular theme. Towards the end of the refrain, Gordan felt a light touch on his shoulder. Looking round quickly, he saw that it was the blonde woman in blue who had been talking to Sir Franklin Marsh.

'Mr. Cross,' she said, bending forward and speaking an urgent whisper, 'Mr. Cross, I must speak to you. I waited until they put the lights down. My name is Destry — Myra Destry.'

'What is it, Miss Destry?' he asked.

'I can't tell you here,' she answered. 'Look, this is my address.' She pushed a piece of paper into his hand. 'Come and see me as soon as you can. It's very urgent.'

'Can't you give me some idea . . . ?' he began, but she interrupted him.

'No, no, not here,' she said with a quick glance round. 'I daren't stop now. Please come as soon as you can . . . tomorrow.' She turned and hurried away.

Gordan leaned across the table towards his wife. 'What do you make of that, Vicky?' he said in a low voice. 'It seems to me that Nosey Williams knew what he was talking about when he suggested I should come to The Yellow Orchid.'

'I wonder what that woman wants to see you about,' she said. 'She sounded very upset.'

'And frightened. Very frightened.'

The number came to an end amid a great deal of applause, and the lights went up. Rodney Mayne bowed several times, smiling, and then disappeared through a curtained arch at the rear of the dais. The band began a slow foxtrot, and soon the dance floor was crowded again.

'That woman's gone,' remarked Vicky, looking round the place. 'I can't see her anywhere. I wonder how she knew your name, Gordan.'

'I don't know. Push over that ashtray, will you, dear?'

She did so, and then she uttered a little exclamation. 'There's something under it,' she said. 'Look, it's a card with something written on it.'

'Slip it into your bag quickly,' he said urgently.

She did so, looking round to see the cause for his sudden change of tone. Two men, accompanied by the head waiter, were making their way towards their table. They were large and well-dressed. The foremost was stout with black very wavy hair, and looked like an Italian. He was the first to reach the table.

With a bow and a smile that revealed a set of very large white teeth, he said: 'Pardon. There eez, I think, a leetle mistake. Theese table . . . '

'What about it?' asked Gordan.

The Italian, for there was no mistaking his nationality, spread his plump white hands. 'I book eet. Earlier theese evening I book it,' he said.

'The head waiter gave it to us,' said Gordan.

'Eet was a mistake.'

'Well, I'm sorry, but — '

'I assure you, Mr. Patrella,' broke in the worried head waiter, 'this was not the table you booked. I've reserved a table for you and Mr. Macbane over there.'

'I book theese table, Henry. I book it on the telephone.'

'That's right,' put in the other man in a slight Scottish accent. 'Number twenty-four was the table booked.'

'And theese is twenty-four,' said Patrella triumphantly, pointing to the small stand of chromium that stood on the table with a card bearing the number. 'See, there.'

'Well,' said Gordan, 'you've got that one over there. What's the difference?'

'I wish for theese one. I always 'ave theese one.'

'Good evening, Patrella,' said a deep, pleasant voice. 'Good evening, Macbane. What's the trouble?' Sir Franklin Marsh had strolled over.

'Sir Franklin,' Patrella said, turning to him excitedly, 'I book these on the telephone. Now I 'ave been given another table.'

'I was told that Mr. Patrella had booked number thirty-four, sir,' explained the head waiter. 'I've reserved that for him.'

'We don't want thirty-four,' grunted Macbane. 'We want this one.'

Sir Franklin bowed to Vicky and bent down to Gordan. 'Would you very much mind moving to the other table?' he said. 'These gentlemen are regular patrons, and they always have this table. I apologize, madam, for any inconvenience.'

'Please don't, Sir Franklin,' said Vicky quickly. 'We don't mind at all, do we, Gordan?'

'No. No,' he said, 'we don't mind in the least.'

'It's exceedingly good of you,' said Sir Franklin. 'I'm really very sorry there should have been a mistake. Show this lady and gentleman to the other table, Henry.'

The head waiter's face expressed relief as Vicky rose and picked up her bag.

'There you are, Mr. Patrella,' said Gordan as he got up too. 'It's all yours. I hope you find everything satisfactory now.'

Patrella was all smiles. His teeth gleamed at them. 'Thank you, thank you — a thousand pardons,' he said. 'I regret to disturb you, but you will understand . . . ?'

'I think I *quite* understand,' said Gordan. 'Come along, darling. Oh, by the way, Sir Franklin, I hope you enjoyed your drink last night?'

Sir Franklin Marsh looked at him blankly. 'My — er — drink?' he repeated.

'At The Blue Feathers in Deptford.'

The other shook his grey head. His face was still blank. 'I'm afraid, sir,' he said, 'you're mistaken. I have no knowledge of the place to which you refer.'

'No?' remarked Gordan. 'Then you really must have a double, Sir Franklin.'

'Yes.' Sir Franklin looked hard at him. 'Yes, it would appear that I must have.'

He stood watching them as they followed Henry to other table. When they were seated and the head waiter had gone, Vicky said: 'Do you think he was lying?'

'Sir Franklin? Yes, I'm sure he was. He did it very well, but I know he was at that pub last night. Vicky, slip that card out of your bag — don't let anybody see you — and give it to me under the table.'

She did so, pretending to powder her nose. Gordan looked at the written message and pursed his lips.

'What does it say?'

''Elsinore Lodge, Barnet. Tonight. Twelve.' And it's signed with the initial 'M'.'

3

Vicky looked across the table at her husband with startled eyes. '"M",' she repeated in a low voice. 'Could that stand for Mr. Midnight?'

Gordan slipped the card into his jacket pocket. 'I should think it's quite probable,' he replied. 'Williams said that he always pays off for a job at midnight, always at different places.'

'And tonight it's this place, Elsinore Lodge. No wonder those two men, Patrella and Macbane, were so anxious to have that table, Gordan.'

'You mean — this message was intended for *them*?' he said. 'Yes . . . yes, I think you're right, darling. Sir Franklin Marsh was very anxious they should have that table, too, wasn't he?'

'Do you mean *he* put the message there?'

'I shouldn't be at all surprised. He's in this business somewhere. What do you make the time?'

She glanced at the little watch on her wrist. 'Not quite half-past ten.'

He sat back and lighted a cigarette. 'Then there's no need to hurry.'

'I suppose that means we're going to Elsinore Lodge?'

He nodded, and blew out a cloud of smoke. 'Yes. I'm curious to see what's supposed to happen there — at twelve o'clock tonight.'

★   ★   ★

Gordan Cross brought the little car to a stop under the overhanging branches of a big chestnut tree. 'We'll leave the car here and walk the rest of the way,' he said. 'It's only about a hundred yards, according to that constable we asked.' He opened the door and got out, turning to help his wife.

'I wonder why he looked at us so strangely,' she remarked.

'I've no idea. Perhaps it was just his natural expression. Keep over in the shadow of these trees, darling. We don't want to be spotted.'

It was a lonely enough place. On either

side of the tree-lined road were meadows and ploughed fields. The wind had risen and sighed mournfully, rustling the leaves, so that the night seemed to be full of whispers.

Vicky, pulling her cloak round her, shivered. 'Ugh!' she said. 'It's horribly cold, darling. My legs are frozen.'

'The wind's changed to the east, I think,' said Gordan. 'It'll keep the rain off, anyway.'

They began to walk up the road, keeping to the rough grass verge. There was no sign of a house, nothing but great clumps of trees and fields.

'We should be getting somewhere near now,' muttered Gordan, peering ahead, 'but I can't see anything like — '

'There's a gateway,' interrupted Vicky. 'Look there — on the other side of the road.'

'That must be it. There's no sign of a house, but it's probably hidden among all those trees.'

They crossed the road. The gate Vicky had seen was set in a high overgrown hedge of privet. It was broken, hanging drunkenly on one hinge, the latch end half buried in the gravel of the drive. On the top bar in faded letters was the name 'Elsinore Lodge'.

'This is the place, anyhow,' whispered Gordan. 'Looks a bit neglected.'

'Gordan,' said Vicky, clutching his arm, 'it's an *empty* house! There's the board — among those trees.'

To one side of the gate, almost hidden by the overhanging trees and the wild growth of the hedge, an estate age board was just discernible.

Gordan pursed his lips in a silent whistle. 'No wonder that policeman looked at us as if we were mad,' he said, 'asking the way to an empty house at this time of night.'

'He might have told us it was empty. What do we do now?'

'Make our way up this drive until we find the house.' Gordan squeezed through between the gate and the post, and Vicky followed him. It was very dark. The driveway curved before them through a tunnel of trees and bushes.

'Be careful how you go,' said Gordan.

'It's overrun with weeds and brambles.'

They picked their way carefully. The path was strewn with trailing briars. The great trees on either side met overhead, their branches swaying and rustling in the rising wind. There were queer little noises in the bushes, as their passing disturbed some night animal, and once there was a great swishing of wings as an owl swooped close to them. A clock, far away and scarcely audible, chimed the quarter before midnight.

The long drive curved in a semicircle. It ended in a clearing, and they saw the house. It was a large gabled building, vague and shadowy against the sky. They stopped and surveyed it.

'It's quite dark and silent,' whispered Vicky.

They could see the porch, a dark smudge, only one degree darker than the bulk of the house, and they went towards it. Gordan was alert, his nerves tense, his ears straining to catch the slightest sound. But except for the sighing of the wind, everything was quite silent.

'The whole place is in a pretty bad state

of repair,' he said. 'Mind you don't fall over these broken steps.'

Vicky's cold fingers slid into his hand. They went up the steps and paused under the great overhanging porch.

And then Gordan made a discovery. The front door was partly open. He pushed it gently, and it moved with a faint creaking sound.

'Gordan . . . you're not going inside?' whispered Vicky.

'Why not? I don't think there's anyone here yet.'

'Somebody must be here, or the door wouldn't be open. Do be careful.'

He nodded. Pushing the door a little wider, he paused and listened. There was no sound from inside.

'I can't hear anything,' he said. 'I'm going in.'

He edged his way round the door in the darkness of the hall, and Vicky followed, her heart beating rapidly. They could see nothing. It was as black as the bottom of a coalmine, but they sensed a vastness that was like illimitable space.

'Keep close to me,' whispered Gordan.

He felt in pocket for his lighter, flicked it on, and shielded the flame with his palm. The light it gave was feeble, but it was sufficient to show him a huge hall with a great carved staircase leading into a cavern of blackness above. Beside the stair was an arch that apparently led to the back portion of the house.

'Listen!' said Vicky suddenly.

'What is it?'

'There's somebody coming up the drive,' she whispered.

He put out the lighter and listened. At first he could hear nothing, and then . . .

It was the faint sound of footsteps on gravel.

'Over there.' He took his wife by the arm and pulled her towards the staircase. 'Down there,' whispered urgently, 'beside the staircase.'

They crouched in the shelter of the massive banisters and waited. The footsteps outside came nearer. When they reached the porch, they stopped. There was a short silence, and then they heard the slow creak of the opening door.

The footsteps came inside, hesitantly

and slowly. The church clock, or whatever it was that they had heard before, began to strike twelve.

There was a pause. Gordan and Vicky waited, scarcely daring to breathe. There came the faint rattle of a match box, followed by the rasping of a match. It flared into a feeble flame and:

'How do you do, Mr. Castell,' said Gordan Cross, rising to his feet. 'Have you brought your band with you?'

4

The man gave a startled exclamation and dropped the match. For a moment the darkness was complete, and then Gordan flicked on his lighter.

Castell blinked at him in evident surprise. 'Who are you?' he demanded. 'What are you doing here?'

'What are *you* doing here?' retorted Gordan.

'I . . . I came to . . . to meet a friend,' stammered Castell. He was uneasy. His eyes kept darting from side to side, searching the shadows as though he expected to see someone spring out.

'You came to meet a friend?' repeated Gordan incredulously. 'In an *empty* house . . . at this time of night?'

'Yes.' Castell was suddenly defiant. 'What business is it of yours, anyway?'

'That depends on who you came to meet.'

'What do you mean?' blustered Castell.

'It wouldn't be a gentleman who calls himself Mr. Midnight by any chance, would it?'

'I don't know what you're talking about.'

'Or perhaps,' went on Gordan easily, '*you're* Mr. Midnight?'

'You're crazy,' snapped Castell impatiently. 'I don't know anybody called Mr. Midnight. Who's he?'

'That's something I'm very curious to know, Mr. Castell. May I inquire what you *did* come here for tonight?'

'I don't recognize your right to question me,' said Castell angrily. 'Who are you?'

'My name is Cross — Gordan Cross.'

'Cross? Cross . . . ?' muttered the other. 'I've seen your name somewhere . . . '

'Possibly in the *Clarion*.'

'That's right — you're a reporter!'

'A *crime* reporter, Mr. Castell.'

'That can have no possible interest for me. I've committed no crime. I came here, as I've already told you, to meet a — a friend.'

The front door behind him swung to and shut with a crash that shook the house. Castell whipped round. 'What was that?' he cried.

'Somebody shut the door,' said Gordan sharply. 'Keep close to me, Vicky!'

'Perhaps it was the wind,' she said doubtfully, and at that moment there was a crash of breaking glass, and something hit the floor with a thud.

'Somebody's thrown a stone or something through the window!' said Castell.

'It's not a stone,' cried Gordan suddenly. 'Run, both of you — through the arch to the back. Go on — as fast as you can!'

They obeyed him. Stumbling along a passage, they almost fell down a short flight of steps, and ended up in a stone-floored kitchen. Gordan found the door and slammed it shut, and almost as he did so, there was a muffled explosion from the direction of the hall.

'Gordan, what was it?' asked Vicky breathlessly.

'A Mills bomb,' he replied grimly. 'I saw it in the light of my lighter.'

'Good God!' said Castell shakily. 'We might have been killed!'

'That was undoubtedly the intention. We'd better get out of here as quickly as possible.' Gordan's lighter had gone out. When he tried to light it again, the wick only glowed redly. 'No petrol,' he said.

'I've got a match,' said Castell. He struck one. They were in a large bare kitchen with a huge rusty range. The floor was covered with litter, and next to the sink was a door. Gordan went over and examined it. It was bolted and festooned with cobwebs. While Castell struck matches, he worked on the bolts, and eventually succeeded in pulling them back. Opening the door, he found, as he had hoped, that it led into the open air.

'Better mind how you go,' he said after a brief inspection. 'It's like a jungle out here.'

They forced their way through creepers, brambles and overgrown bushes. Presently they struck a path. It was ankle-deep in weeds, but was just distinguishable.

'It probably leads round to the main

drive,' said Gordan. 'Be careful; some-body may still be lurking about.'

'I don't understand,' said Castell. 'What — ?'

'Never mind that now,' interrupted Gordan. 'Let's get away from here as quickly as possible. It's not a very healthy neighbourhood.'

The overgrown path came out, as he had expected, into the main drive. As they pushed their way through a tangled mass of foliage and emerged, Vicky uttered an exclamation. 'Look,' she cried, 'what's that light?'

They looked back towards the house. From the darkness of the screening trees, a flicker of light showed fitfully, waxing and waning.

'Great Caesar!' muttered Gordan. 'The explosion must have set the place on fire. Come on, we'd better give the alarm.'

He led the way down the drive with the others at his heels.

'An evening gown isn't the best thing for this sort of life,' panted Vicky. 'Oh!' She gave a little squeal.

'What's the matter?' asked Gordan.

'Something with thorns. Oh, Gordan — my new nylons!'

'Never mind that now, darling,' he said impatiently.

'But they're ruined,' she protested plaintively. 'The last good pair I had.'

'Keep on the grass edging,' he said, 'close to the shrubbery.'

They were nearing the broken gate when a faint sound reached them.

'What was that?' asked Castell.

'It sounded like someone in pain,' answered Gordan. He stopped and listened. The sound came again. This time there was no mistaking it. It was a groan. It came from somewhere among the bushes at the side of the drive.

Gordan tried to locate the spot. 'Over there, I think,' he said, and plunged in amongst thickly growing bushes. Beyond, there was a small clearing, and in the middle of it he saw something white. It moved slightly, and once more there was a moan of pain.

'Gordan,' cried Vicky over his shoulder, 'it's a woman!'

'She's badly hurt from the sound of it,'

44

said Gordan. He dropped to his knees beside her. 'Castell,' he called sharply, 'strike a match.'

Castell bent forward. The match rasped on the box a broke into a feeble flame.

'Oh, look!' breathed Vicky. 'There's blood on her dress!'

'She's been stabbed,' muttered Gordan. 'Castell, bring that light nearer.'

It was the woman who had spoken to him at The Yellow Orchid — Myra Destry.

★   ★   ★

Vicky came out of the little kitchen with a percolator of fresh coffee and set it on the breakfast table. In spite of the fact that it had been in the small hours of the morning before she had got to bed, she looked very fresh in her blue housecoat.

A burst of singing from the bathroom at the end of the tiny passage indicated the whereabouts of her husband. She went back into the kitchen and turned the gas down in the oven where the breakfast was keeping hot. Then she walked resolutely to the bathroom door and knocked.

'Gordan,' she called. 'Gordan . . . '

There was no reply. The singing continued, accompanied by loud splashing.

'Gordan,' she repeated in a higher key. 'How long are you going to be? Breakfast's ready.'

But the singing and the splashing continued unabated. Impatiently, Vicky banged loudly on the door. 'Gordan Cross,' she cried, 'for goodness sake, stop that noise.'

The singer stopped abruptly in the middle of a particularly unmusical note. 'I was only singing,' answered her husband in an aggrieved tone.

'I shouldn't think even the Greeks had a word for it,' she said. 'Do hurry up. The breakfast will be ruined.'

'I'll be with you in a jiffy,' he called. 'Ow!' There was a thud, a loud splash, and a yell of pain.

'Now what have you done?'

'Slipped on the soap.'

'Do stop playing about, Gordan,' said

46

Vicky, unimpressed. 'And hurry up. I want my breakfast.'

There was a knock on the front door, and she frowned. 'Who can *that* be?' she muttered under her breath as she went to open the door.

A very fat sleepy-eyed man stood on the doorstep. 'Good mornin', Mrs. Cross,' he murmured gently.

'Hello, Mr. Budd,' said Vicky. 'Come in.'

'Thank you, m'am,' said Superintendent Budd. 'I hope I'm not bein' a nuisance?'

'Of course not.' She closed the door behind his portly figure and led the way into the dining-room. 'I suppose you want to see Gordan? He's still in the bath.'

'Ah,' murmured Mr. Budd. 'I don't s'pose you got to bed very early?'

'As a matter of fact we did,' said Vicky. 'Very early this morning.'

'Ah,' remarked the big man again.

'I'll tell Gordan you're here. Please, sit down.'

Mr. Budd lowered himself ponderously into a chair, and she went and hammered once more on the bathroom door. 'Gordan, Mr. Budd's here!' she called.

'Budd?' shouted Gordan. 'All right — I'll be out in a minute.'

She went back to the dining-room. 'Would you like some coffee?' she asked. 'I've just made it.'

'Well now, that's very nice of you, Mrs. Cross,' said Mr. Budd.

'Gordan won't be long, I hope,' she said as she began to pour out the coffee.

Mr. Budd looked at her sleepily. 'You 'ad quite an excitin' time last night, eh, Mrs Cross?'

'Yes; a little too exciting at one point,' she replied. 'Help yourself to sugar.' She set the cup of coffee in front of him and pushed over the sugar bowl. He took a large spoonful and stirred the coffee methodically.

'Thank you,' he said. 'I 'aven't got all the details yet; only what your husband told the local police. That's why I'm 'ere. I expect Mr. Cross can add quite a lot to what he's already said in 'is statement. One thin' I'd like ter — '

'Good morning, Budd,' broke in

Gordan Cross cheerily, coming quickly in, wrapped in a bathrobe. 'So you're in on this business, are you?'

'Good mornin', Mr. Cross,' said the big man. 'I'm inquirin' into the murder o' this woman, Myra Destry, if that's what yer mean.'

'I'm glad they've put you in charge of it,' said Gordan. He sat down. 'You don't mind if I eat while we talk?' he added as Vicky brought in a dish of eggs and bacon.

'Go ahead,' said Mr. Budd.

'Would you like some too?' inquired Gordan as he filled his wife's plate.

'No, thank you,' said Mr. Budd. 'I 'ad me breakfast nearly three hours ago.'

'That's lucky,' remarked Vicky, 'because we haven't any more eggs and bacon.'

'Oh, haven't we, darling?' said Gordan. 'Well, you could have always have given him yours.' He gulped some coffee. 'Now, what do you want to know, Budd?'

'Everythin' you didn't put in that statement o' yours,' said Mr. Budd. 'What was you an' Mrs. Cross doin' at that empty house in Barnet in the middle of the night?'

'Have you ever heard of Mr. Midnight?' asked Gordan with his mouth full.

The big man shook his head slowly. 'Can't say I 'ave. Who is 'e?'

'I wish I knew,' said the reporter. 'I'm most anxious to meet him. He's the man who killed Myra Destry.'

'Oh, 'ow do you know that?' Mr. Budd was suddenly very wide awake.

'Because she told me,' answered Gordan quietly.

The big man stared at him. '*She* told you?' he repeated.

'She wasn't quite dead when we found her. She lived for a few seconds — long enough to whisper the name Midnight and something about a ring — an Intaglio ring.'

'An Intaglio ring?' Mr. Budd looked puzzled.

'Yes. I think she was trying to give me a clue to the identity of Mr. Midnight.'

'You didn't mention any of this in your statement,' said Mr. Budd accusingly.

'No, I didn't,' admitted Gordan, 'and I shouldn't mention it now if it were anyone else but you. You see, the murder of Myra Destry is only a side issue. She was killed because she knew something.'

'About what?' asked Mr. Budd.

'About this man, Mr. Midnight.' Gordan reached for the toast. 'She knew something, and she was going to tell me what she knew. That's why she died, Budd. Because she knew too much.'

5

Mr. Budd drank his coffee noisily and set down the empty cup. 'Who's this feller Mr. Midnight you keep talking about?' he asked.

'You know the epidemic of robberies that's broken out in the last few months — lorries stolen, warehouses broken into, shops raided?'

The superintendent sniffed. 'If you're tryin' ter tell me,' he said scornfully, 'that it's the work of an organized gang . . . '

'I'm not. But I believe all stolen stuff is handled by one man working through a central depot.'

'A sort of super-fence, eh?' remarked Mr. Budd.

'Exactly.'

'Hm, there might be somethin' in that, Mr. Cross. I don't mind admittin' that we've 'ad the same idea at the Yard. You think this feller you call Mr. Midnight is the big noise?'

'Nosey Williams says he is.'

'Williams, eh?' Mr. Budd pursed his lips. 'Well, 'is information's usually pretty reliable. I wonder why 'e hasn't said anythin' to us.'

'Because he's scared to the teeth. I had to drag it out of him under threats.'

'But he didn't say who the feller was?'

'No, he says he doesn't know.'

'D'you think he's tellin' the truth?'

Gordan shrugged his shoulders. 'I don't know. He won't squeal, anyway.'

'Queer alias, ain't it?' remarked Mr. Budd. ''Ow did 'e come by it?'

'According to Williams, because that's the time he always pays out — midnight, and never at the same place twice. I thought Elsinore Lodge was the place chosen for last night.'

'I see,' murmured the big man. 'So *that*'s what you was doin' there, eh? What made you think Elsinore Lodge was the place?'

'Something that happened earlier at The Yellow Orchid, that new roadhouse near St. Albans,' explained Vicky. 'A very nice place.'

'On the surface, anyway,' put in Gordan. 'I'm not sure that it's so nice underneath. It was Nosey who suggested I should go there.'

'That's where we first saw Myra Destry,' said Vicky. She told him how they had first met the woman. 'I thought she seemed — well, rather scared.'

'Apparently she 'ad good cause to be,' grunted Mr. Budd. 'This feller, Castell, who was with yer . . . ?'

'He's the band leader at The Yellow Orchid,' said Vicky.

'Is he?' remarked Mr. Budd. 'Well, well — this Yellow Orchid place seems ter figure pretty prominently, don't it? What was 'e doin' at Elsinore Lodge?'

'He said he had an appointment to meet Myra Destry there.'

'Queer time to choose to meet 'is girlfriend,' murmured the big man. 'Queer place, too.'

'That's what I thought,' said Gordan. 'He says she rang him up at The Yellow Orchid and said she *must* see him — it was very urgent. He says he had no idea it was an empty house.'

54

'an' when 'e got there,' murmured Mr. Budd, 'somebody chucked a Mills bomb through the hall winder. Hm.'

'Yes — somebody arranged it very cleverly, don't you think?' remarked Gordan.

Vicky looked at him, her eyes wide. 'You don't mean . . . ?'

'That Mills bomb was intended for Castell *and* Myra Destry,' he said. 'Unfortunately for the plan, she was late and had to be dealt with differently.'

'Then the message that Castell got was a fake?' said Mr. Budd.

'Of course,' agreed Gordan. 'I believe Myra Destry got a message, too, purporting to be from Castell.'

'Maybe you've got somethin' there, Mr. Cross,' said Mr. Budd thoughtfully. 'I suppose you're workin' on this for the *Clarion*?'

'Yes. Can I have some more coffee, darling?'

She poured it out. 'Would you like some more, Mr. Budd?' she asked.

'No, thank you, Mrs. Cross,' he said. 'Who owns this Yellow Orchid, d'yer know?'

'A man named Franklin Marsh,' answered Gordan. '*Sir* Franklin Marsh.'

'Sir Franklin Marsh, eh? Now that's very interestin' — very interestin' indeed.'

'Why? Do you know anything about him?' asked Gordan.

'Only,' said Mr. Budd slowly, 'that he's also the owner of that 'ouse at Barnet where Myra Destry was murdered.'

'Are you sure?' asked Gordan.

'Yes,' answered Mr. Budd. 'The place 'as been empty for a long time. Badly damaged by a bomb fallin' near durin' the war.'

'And even worse damaged by the bomb that fell last night,' said Gordan. 'The fire brigade did their best, but they couldn't — '

The telephone rang.

'I'll answer it,' said Vicky. She got up and went over to the instrument. 'Hello?' she said. 'Yes . . . yes . . . Oh, hello. Sergeant Leek . . . yes, he is . . . Just a minute.' She turned and looked at Mr. Budd. 'It's for you,' she said.

He rose ponderously to his feet, went over, and took the receiver from her hand. 'What is it, Leek?'

The telephone chattered excitedly.

'What!' exclaimed the big man. 'All right, yes . . . wait there for me. I'll come straight along.' He banged the receiver back on its rack. 'What time did Castell leave you this mornin'?' he asked.

'About two-fifteen, wasn't it, Vicky?' said Gordan.

'Yes,' she replied. 'He said he was going home.'

'He never reached there,' said Mr. Budd grimly. 'Leek was phonin' from his flat. He 'asn't been 'ome all night, an' his car was found an hour ago on a lonely stretch of road near Barnet — empty!'

'Good Lord!' exclaimed Gordan. 'What can have happened to him?'

'I don't know, Mr. Cross.' The superintendent shook his head. 'But I don't like the look of it. I'm goin' round to 'is flat now. Leek's waitin' there for me.'

'Can I come?' asked Gordan quickly.

'You'll 'ave ter hurry,' said Mr. Budd, looking at the bathrobe.

'I won't be a minute,' declared Gordan, and he made a dash for the bedroom.

★ ★ ★

57

Laddie Castell lived in a large block of flats in Kensington. It was an expensive-looking place with sun blinds and window-boxes. Vicky surveyed it with approval as the car drew up in front of the entrance. 'Quite a nice-looking place,' she said.

'Not bad,' agreed Gordan. 'What's the number of Castell's flat, Budd?'

'Eighty-seven,' answered the big man. 'You can 'ave all these blocks o' flats for me. Give me a little 'ouse with a bit o' garden where you can grow things.' He got carefully out of the car and looked about. 'Leek should be somewhere.'

'There he is,' said Vicky, 'just inside the vestibule.'

'Who's that 'e's talkin' to?'

Gordan supplied him with the answer, rather to his surprise. 'That,' he said, 'is a gentleman called Rodney Mayne. He's the singer with Castell's band.'

Mr. Budd made no comment. He walked slowly over to Leek, the others following him. The lean sergeant came to meet him.

'Well,' said Mr. Budd, 'anythin' fresh?'

58

Leek shook his head. 'Nuthin',' he replied in his melancholy voice. 'I'm feelin' tired out an' — '

'You never feel anythin' else,' growled his superior. 'No sign of Castell?'

'No, he ain't in 'is flat and 'e ain't been back. I've 'ad a word with the porter. Castell always leaves 'is key under the mat for the lady what looks after 'im ter come in an' get 'is breakfast an' clean up. There was no key there this mornin', an' she couldn't get any answer when she knocked.'

'Hm. Go along an' see if the porter's got a passkey,' ordered Mr. Budd.

'We ain't got no right, yer know, without a warrant,' said Leek, but Mr. Budd cut him short.

'I'll take the responsibility for that. This may be serious.' He looked at the good-looking young man to whom Leek had been talking. 'Your name's Rodney Mayne, isn't it?'

'Yes.' Mayne seemed surprised. 'How did you — '

'We heard you sing at The Yellow Orchid last night,' put in Vicky.

59

Mayne's face cleared. 'Oh, I see,' he said.

'Did you come here to see Castell this morning?' asked Gordan.

'Yes, I had an appointment.' Mayne looked from one to the other, and the worried expression returned. 'I say, what's all the trouble about?'

'We don't know — yet,' answered Mr. Budd. 'What was your business with Mr. Castell?'

'He wanted me to try over a new number.'

'Did he arrange this appointment with you last night at The Yellow Orchid?' said Gordan.

Mayne nodded. 'Yes, just before he got the telephone message.'

'The message from Miss Destry?'

'Well . . . I believe it was from Miss Destry.' Mayne was hesitant. 'Look here, what's the matter?'

'Something rather serious, I'm afraid,' replied Gordan. 'Ah, here comes the porter.'

A small wiry man approached them with Leek. His was a mass of wrinkles, and his short hair was grey, with skin the colour of mahogany. From the tattoo on his arm, Gordan judged him to be a retired sailor.

'Yer want me to let you inter Mr. Castell's flat, sir?' he said, addressing Mr. Budd.

'Yes,' said the big man. 'Can you do that?'

'Well, I *can*, but I don't know as I oughter. Yer see, I'm responsible like, an' well, 'ow do I know that — '

Mr. Budd produced his warrant card. 'Take a look at that,' he said, holding it under the porter's nose. 'Maybe that'll reassure yer.'

'I s'pose it's all right,' said the porter reluctantly, 'seein' as yer from Scotland Yard.'

'Scotland Yard?' said Mayne softly, almost to himself.

'The lift's just round the corner,' went on the porter. 'I'll take yer up.'

'Come along with us, Mr. Mayne, will you?' said Mr. Budd as they followed the porter to the lift.

'Yes, certainly.' Mayne was evidently

61

puzzled and curious.

The lift took them up swiftly. The porter opened the door and escorted them along a corridor. At a door near the far end, he stopped.

''Ere yer are,' he said. He produced a pass-key from his pocket and inserted it in the lock.

'Gordan,' whispered Vicky as a sudden possibility struck her, 'you don't think that . . . ' She paused.

'What, darling?'

'That Castell *is* there?'

He guessed what she meant, and shook his head. 'No, I don't think so.'

With the key in the lock, the porter hesitated. 'If there's any trouble comes o' this,' he said, looking up at Mr. Budd, 'you'll see that I'm . . . ?'

'Yes, yes,' broke in the big man impatiently. 'Go on, open the door.'

The porter turned the key and pushed open the door. They went into a square comfortably furnished hall. On the carpet inside the front door lay several letters. Mr. Budd pointed at them.

'Pick 'em up, Leek,' he ordered. 'They

prove that Castell didn't come 'ome last night.'

''Ere, this is funny,' exclaimed the lean sergeant, looking at the letters. 'One o' these is addressed ter you, Mr. Cross.'

'To me?' said Gordan in surprise.

'Yes. It ain't come through the post neither. There's no stamp on it.'

'Open it and see what it says,' said Vicky.

Gordan took it and slid his thumb under the flap of the envelope.

6

From the open envelope, Gordan withdrew a single sheet of paper.

'What does it say?' asked Vicky impatiently.

''I wonder if you realize just what you're up against,'' Gordan read the message aloud. ''The person known as Mr. Midnight is quite ruthless, Mr. Cross, as you should be aware by now. It will be interesting to see if you survive.' The signature is 'A. Smith'.'

'Who's 'A. Smith'?' asked Mr. Budd.

Gordan shook his head. 'I haven't the vaguest idea. Oh, there's a postscript on the other side. 'A visit to Evesham Mansions should prove interesting.''

'That's the address Myra Destry gave you,' said Vicky.

'Yes; I wonder if the writer of this note knows that she's dead.'

'*Dead?*' The horrified exclamation came from Mayne.

'She was murdered last night,' said Gordan.

'Murdered! *Myra?* Good God — you don't mean that Castell — ' Mayne stopped suddenly.

'Go on, Mr. Mayne,' said Mr. Budd softly. 'That Castell — what?'

'Well . . . I thought . . . you see, you're from Scotland Yard, and . . . ' Mayne broke off in confusion.

'You thought Castell might 'ave killed her,' said Mr. Budd. 'Is that what you thought, Mr. Mayne?'

Mayne flushed. 'Well he's not here, and the . . . the police seem to be looking for him . . . ' He was all but incoherent. 'For the moment I suppose I did think something of the sort.'

'You hadn't any other reason for thinking so, Mr. Mayne?' asked Mr. Budd.

Mayne shook his head vigorously. 'No . . . no, of course not!'

Leek, who had opened a door at the end of the hall, turned and called excitedly: 'I say — come an' look in 'ere, will yer?'

65

'What is it?' asked Mr. Budd.

'Come an' look,' said Leek, and the big man waddled over to him. 'Take a look at that,' invited the sergeant.

Mr. Budd whistled softly. Gordan and Vicky, who had followed him, peered over his shoulder into the room beyond.

It was comfortably furnished — at least, it had been. Now it looked as though a gale had struck it. The pictures were askew and the cushions of the big chairs lay scattered on the floor, some of them ripped open. Books had been taken from the shelves and flung on the floor. Open drawers spilled their contents, and even the carpet had been turned back.

'Holy smoke!' exclaimed Gordan. 'Somebody appears to have been pretty busy.'

'Nasty mess they've made o' the place, ain't they?' remarked Leek.

'Yes, they've even ripped the back out of the settee,' said the reporter. 'I wonder what they were looking for.'

'D'you think the rest of the flat's the same?' said Mr. Budd. He turned and opened another door that faced the first. The room was a bedroom, and here, too, were signs of the searcher. The bed was stripped, the sheets and covers strewn all over the floor. A wardrobe had been denuded of its contents; and shirts, socks, underclothes and handkerchiefs rioted over the floor. The window curtains had been torn down and a suitcase broken open.

'What could they 'ave been lookin' for?' muttered Mr. Budd, surveying the mess and confusion through half-closed eyes.

'Did they find it?' said Gordan. 'That's the question.'

'an' we can't answer it,' said Mr. Budd, 'because we don't know what it was. What's the rest o' the place like?'

They made a tour of inspection. The intruder had not overlooked anywhere. The tiny kitchen, the bathroom, a spare bedroom, all had suffered from his attentions. Only the hall had escaped, and that was probably because there was nowhere anything could have been hidden.

'Well,' remarked Mr. Budd when they had completed their tour of the flat, 'whoever it was, they was thorough. The place has been gone through with a fine-toothed comb. 'Ow do you s'pose they got in?'

'That's easy,' said Gordan seriously. 'They used the key, Budd — the key they took from Laddie Castell.'

★ ★ ★

Evesham Mansions was a large block of flats in St. John's Wood. Although Conway Court, where Castell had lived, was something special in the way of flats, Evesham Mansions was the last word.

'Myra Destry must have been very well off to have lived in a place like this,' said Vicky as they crossed the pavement to the main entrance. 'I shouldn't think any of these flats were less than eight hundred a year.'

'Yes,' murmured her husband. 'I wonder where the money came from.'

'Maybe we'll be able to answer that when we've found out a bit more about 'er,' said Mr. Budd. He look sleepily round the luxurious vestibule. 'I'll go an' have a word with the porter.'

'Wait a minute,' said Gordan. 'A

woman who could afford to live in one of these flats would probably keep a maid, don't you think, Vicky?'

She nodded. 'I should think it's almost a certainty.'

'In which case, she won't know yet that anything has happened to her mistress,' went on Gordan. 'We might get some useful information out of her.'

'That's not a bad idea, Mr. Cross,' agreed the big man. 'Anyway, it's worth tryin'.'

'Come on, then,' said Gordan. 'Her flat should be on the ground floor.'

He led the way along a corridor that was paved with carpet so thick that it was like walking on a well-kept lawn. Concealed lighting shed a soft golden radiance from behind the cornice, and the front doors to the various flats were of polished walnut.

'I wonder what 'A. Smith' meant by 'a visit here would prove interesting',' remarked Vicky as they searched for number eight, which was the number the dead woman had given Gordan when she had spoken to him in The Yellow Orchid.

'I'm rather curious about that, too,' said Gordan.

'I'm more curious about 'A. Smith' 'imself,' grunted Mr. Budd. 'Who is 'e, an' why did he write that note to you an' leave it at Castell's flat? 'Ow did 'e know you'd go there?'

'Your guess is as good as mine,' said Gordan. 'Here we are — eight.' He stopped at a door above which, inset in a small glass panel illuminated behind, was a black figure eight. Flush with the wall at the side of the door was an ivory bell-push. Gordan pressed it, and they heard muted chimes ring inside. 'Let me handle this,' he said in a low voice.

Mr. Budd nodded. 'Go ahead.'

The door opened suddenly, and a woman looked inquiringly at them. She was a very attractive dark woman in her early thirties, Gordan guessed, and dressed in a house-frock of jade-green velvet.

'What is it?' she asked curtly. Her voice was slightly common, just the hint of a harshness that grated.

'Good morning,' said Gordan. 'Does Miss Destry live here?'

'You mean Mrs. Destry,' she answered. 'What do you want?'

'Is she at home?' asked Gordan.

'She is,' said the woman coolly. '*I* am Mrs. Destry.'

'We're looking for *Myra* Destry,' said Vicky.

'Well, you don't need to look very far. *I'm* Myra Destry.'

They were taken aback for a moment. This woman with the black hair who was looking at them with a rather bored expression in her heavy-lidded eyes was as unlike the Myra Destry who had spoken to Gordan Cross in The Yellow Orchid, and later been stabbed to death in the shrubbery at Elsinore Lodge, as it was possible for two people to be.

'I'm afraid there must be some mistake,' he said. 'The person we're looking for is fair — very fair.'

'The mistake is yours, isn't it?' said the woman. 'I'm Myra Destry, and I'm a brunette, as you can see.'

'What is it, Myra?' A man had come softly up behind her, making no noise on the thick carpet. He was tall and

71

good-looking. Beneath his thin nose, a streak of moustache lay across his upper lip.

'These people are looking for someone called Myra Destry, Richard,' she said over her shoulder.

'Well, that's you.'

'But it isn't,' she said. 'Their Myra Destry is a blonde.'

'No blonde here,' he announced cheerfully. 'You've come to the wrong address.'

'This is the address we were given,' said Gordan. 'Eight Evesham Mansions.'

'Somebody must have made a mistake,' said the man, shaking his head. 'My wife is the only Myra Destry in these flats.'

'You 'aven't a sister, sir, have you?' said Mr. Budd gently.

Richard Destry laughed. 'No. And even if I had, it would be a very strange coincidence if her Christian name were the same as my wife's, wouldn't it?'

'Yes,' murmured Gordan Cross, 'yes, it would.'

'You must have got the address mixed up.'

'It certainly looks like it,' agreed Gordan. 'I'm very sorry to have bothered you, Mrs. — er — Destry.'

'Oh, don't worry about that,' she said quickly. 'I hope you find your friend.'

'It's odd that she should have the same name as my wife,' said Destry.

'Very odd,' said Gordan.

There was a moment's silence.

'Well, sorry we can't help you,' said Destry.

His wife began to close the door. 'Good-bye,' she said.

The door shut, and they looked at each other.

'Well,' said Vicky in a low voice, 'what do you make of that?'

'You're sure this was the address, Mr. Cross?' asked Mr. Budd.

'Quite sure,' answered Gordan.

'There's no doubt about that,' said Vicky. 'Eight Evesham Mansions was the address Myra Destry gave us.'

'Well,' declared the big man, scratching his chin, 'I don't understand it.'

'Neither do I,' said Gordan, frowning.

'I suppose the dead woman's name *was*

73

Destry?' said Mr. Budd. 'There was nothing on the body to identify her.'

'She said that was her name,' said Vicky.

'The waiter at The Yellow Orchid said it was, too,' said Gordan. 'Castell recognized her as well.'

'She may have only *called* herself Myra Destry,' suggested Mr. Budd.

'But she gave me this address and asked me to come and see her,' said Gordan.

'Listen,' said Vicky suddenly, 'supposing it's those two — ' She jerked her head towards the closed door of number eight. ' — whose names aren't Destry?'

'That's easily settled, Mrs. Cross,' said Mr. Budd. 'I'll go an' 'ave a word with the porter. 'E'll be able ter tell us.'

They began to walk back towards the vestibule. As they passed one of the flats, the front door opened and a man came out. Vicky caught her husband's sleeve.

'Look, Gordan,' she whispered. 'That man who's just come out of that flat.'

'Mr. Patrella,' said Gordan. 'Is he a resident here? Good morning, Mr. Patrella.'

The man swung round. Recognition flickered in his eyes — recognition and uneasiness.

'I do not think that I — ' he began, but Gordan wasn't going to let him get away with it.

'We met last night at The Yellow Orchid,' he said easily.

'Ah yes, of course. I remember,' said Patrella reluctantly. 'There was some mistake about the table. That was it, yes?'

'That was it.'

'You must forgive me for 'aving been so insistent,' said Patrella with a great display of teeth. 'It eese, 'ow you put it, a habit with me. I must always 'ave the same table, you understand?'

'Yes,' said Gordan significantly. 'I understand very well, Mr. Patrella.'

'Do you live here?' asked Vicky.

'Yes, I live 'ere, at number five. It eese a nice place, yes? Very convenient.'

'I'm sure it is,' said Gordan. 'Have you lived here long?'

Patrella wrinkled his forehead. 'Six . . . seven . . . nine months,' he said. 'Not really very long.'

'I suppose you know a good many of the other tenants?' said Vicky.

'One or two. Not many.'

'Do you happen to know a woman called Myra Destry?' inquired Gordan.

It might have been his imagination, but he thought he saw a wary look come into the other's eyes. 'Myra Destry?' he repeated.

'She was at The Yellow Orchid last night,' said Vicky.

'I do not know all the women who go to The Yellow Orchid.' Patrella spread his hands. 'Why do you ask?'

'We were told she had a flat here,' said Gordan.

'Number eight, Mr. Patrella,' said Vicky.

'Number eight?' Patrella pulled at his lower lip. 'Ah, yes,' he exclaimed suddenly, 'there are some people living there called Destry, I believe. But the lady is dark. She cannot be the woman you want.'

'Why not, Patrella?' asked Gordan quickly.

The man realized he had made a slip, and did his best to cover it up. 'Well, of course, I do not know,' he said. 'I only

76

imagined that this woman you speak of was a blonde.'

'It was a remarkable piece of imagination,' remarked Gordan. 'You're quite right.'

'Patrella — Patrella . . . ' A man came hurrying in from the vestibule. It was Macbane.

'You will excuse?' said Patrella hurriedly. 'My friend, he is impatient.'

'Mr. Macbane, isn't it?' said Vicky.

'Yes.' Patrella looked surprised, and then his face cleared. 'Of course; he was with me last night.'

'Hurry up, Patrella,' called Macbane. 'We'll be late.'

'I'm coming.' He bowed to Vicky. '*Addio.*'

'*Arrivederci,*' she said.

They watched the two men hurry away. When they had gone, Vicky turned to her husband. 'He does know Myra Destry, Gordan,' she said excitedly. 'I'm sure he does.'

'So am I,' he replied. 'That was a pretty bad slip he made.'

'Did you notice he said she was a blonde?'

He nodded. 'It looks as though he

knew she was dead, doesn't it? Hello, here comes Budd back again.'

Mr. Budd had left them to find the porter when they had stopped to speak to Patrella. He came up to them, breathing a little heavily, his fat face redder than ever. 'Who was that feller you was speakin' to?' he inquired.

'I'll tell you later,' said Gordan. 'What did you get out of the porter?'

'Those people in number eight are quite genuine, apparently,' said the big man. 'The woman's name *is* Myra Destry, an' they've been living in that flat for over year.'

'Then who was the woman at The Yellow Orchid?' said Vicky.

Mr. Budd shook his head wearily. 'That's what I'd like to know, Mrs. Cross. The porter told me somethin' else that was queer. This block o' flats belonged to a company — the Evesham Estate Company Limited. Six months ago they sold it lock, stock and barrel. Who do you think bought it?'

'I've no idea,' said Gordan. 'Who?'

'Sir Franklin Marsh.'

7

'Black or white coffee, sir?' asked the waitress.

'Eh?' said Gordan, looking up with a start. 'Oh — er — black, please.'

'I'll have white,' said Vicky, and when the woman had gone: 'Do you know that's practically the first word you've spoken all through lunch?'

He took out his cigarette case and offered it to her. 'You made up for both of us,' he remarked. 'You've never stopped! I couldn't have got a word in edgeways if I'd wanted to.'

'Well, I like that,' she said indignantly.

'I know you do. But it's very distracting when I'm trying to think.'

She took a cigarette. 'Why attempt the impossible, darling?' she said sweetly. 'May I have a light?'

He took out his lighter, flicked it into flame, and held it out to her. 'You should have a saucer of milk instead of coffee,' he said.

'Thank you, darling.'

They were sitting in a small restaurant in Knightsbridge. Mr. Budd had gone back to the Yard, leaving them to their own resources, and hunger had suggested the obvious. All through lunch, Gordan had been lost in thought, merely grunting in reply to the spate of words his wife had poured out.

'Where,' she asked, blowing a cloud of smoke gently across the table, 'has this vast amount of thought got you?'

'Not very far, I'm afraid,' he admitted. He helped himself to a cigarette and lit it absently. 'You know, Vicki, the whole thing's very queer.'

'Surely it didn't require a very great mental effort to reach that conclusion.'

He ignored her remark. 'If that woman, Myra Destry, really had something important to tell me, why on earth give me an address that wouldn't find her? It doesn't make sense!'

'Perhaps it would have made sense if she hadn't been killed. You think she knew who Mr. Midnight is?'

'No, I don't think she actually knew his

80

identity. If she had, she'd have told me before she died. Instead, she did the best she could.'

'When she said something about an Intaglio ring . . . '

'Yes . . . ?'

'Does that mean that to find Mr. Midnight we've got look for somebody who wears that type of ring?'

'Probably, but not necessarily. There may be some other connection. She was trying to give me clue that would lead to him.'

Vicky flicked the ash off her cigarette. 'She must have had some good reason for giving you that address at Evesham Mansions.'

'Can you think of one?'

'No — unless she really *did* live there.'

'That seems to be impossible. The porter was positive that the Destrys have had no one staying with them. He said he'd have seen them going in and out. Besides, doesn't explain why she adopted the name of Myra Destry.'

'No, it's all very strange,' said Vicky, frowning. 'She must have been known by it for a long time.'

'Yes. Castell knew her as Myra Destry. So did that waiter and Rodney Mayne.'

'And Patrella,' added Vicky. 'Gordan, Castell must have known her real address.'

'Possibly, but I'm very much afraid he won't be able to tell us.'

'You think he's dead?' she asked quickly.

'Yes — there's not much doubt in my opinion about that.' He stopped abruptly. A curious expression came into his eyes.

'You've thought of something?' said Vicky. 'What is it?'

'Just an idea that came to me,' he replied evasively. 'I say, what do you think has happened to our coffee?'

'Don't you dare to change the subject. What did you suddenly think of just now?'

'Here comes the waitress.'

The woman came up with a tray. She set down three cups of coffee, and Gordan raised his eyebrows. 'You've made a mistake,' he said. 'Why three cups?'

'The lady over there said she'd be

joining you,' said the woman.

'Lady? Which lady?' asked Gordan in surprise.

'The one at the table near the window.' The waitress turned. 'Oh, here she comes now, sir.'

Gordan followed the direction of her eyes. An attractive, very smartly dressed woman was approaching their table. She was quite young, and as she saw him looking at her, she smiled.

'Who is it?' asked Vicky suspiciously.

'I don't know,' answered her husband. 'I've never seen her before in my life.'

The woman came up and stopped. Gordan rose. 'Don't get up, Mr. Cross,' she said in a pleasant voice. 'I'll sit down, if I may?'

'Of course.' A little bewildered, but curious, he pulled out a chair. She sat down, a mischievous little twinkle in her eyes.

'I hope you and your wife will forgive my intrusion,' she said.

'I'm afraid I don't know who — ' began Gordan.

'Naturally,' she interrupted him. 'We've

never met before. Let me introduce myself. My name is Smith. A. Smith.'

Gordan stared at her in almost open-mouthed astonishment. So completely taken aback was he that it was several seconds before he found his voice.

'You — you're 'A. Smith'?' he stammered at last.

Her eyes twinkled as she nodded calmly. 'Yes, I'm 'A. Smith'. The 'A.' stands for Audrey.'

Gordan swallowed with difficulty. His throat felt suddenly dry. 'Did you write that note? The one addressed to me in Castell's flat?'

'Try a little coffee,' she suggested. 'You sound a trifle husky.'

He took a quick sip from his cup. 'Did you write that note?' he repeated.

'I did.'

He took out a packet of Players, offered a cigarette to her and Vicky, and took one himself. He felt that he needed the soothing effect of tobacco very badly. 'What do you know about Mr. Midnight?' he asked, holding out his lighter.

She leaned forward and dipped the end

of her cigarette in the tiny flame. 'Just a little more than you do, I think,' she said, blowing a thin stream of smoke from between her lips.

He lit Vicky's cigarette and his own, and put the lighter back in his pocket. 'You wouldn't have to know a lot for that,' he said. 'Tell me what you *do* know.'

She shook her head. 'Oh, no — I've no intention of doing that.'

He looked at her in surprise. 'I don't quite understand.'

She returned his look coolly, one eyebrow slightly raised. 'I didn't come here to tell you what *I* know,' she said. 'I came to find out what *you* know.'

'Can you give me any valid reason why I should tell you?'

'No, I can't. There is one, but you'll have to take my word for it.'

Gordan drew in the smoke of his cigarette and inhaled deeply. For sheer consummate nerve, he thought, this woman who called herself 'A. Smith' would be hard to beat. She seemed to read his thoughts.

'You think that's rather an audacious

request, don't you?' she said.

'I do, in the circumstances. This isn't a game, you know. It's serious. A murder has been committed — maybe more than one.'

'You mean Laddie Castell?'

'Yes. I think it very unlikely that he's still alive.'

'So do I. You're wrong if you think I don't realize how serious it is.'

'If you do,' said Gordan quickly, 'you ought to tell us anything you know.'

'I can't,' she answered, and there was sincerity in her voice. 'I can't, Mr. Cross. I've got to keep out of this.'

'Then why did you write that note?' asked Vicky.

'Because I thought the hint about Evesham Mansions might be useful.'

'Did you know what we were going to find there?' asked Gordan.

'Do you mean the Destrys?'

'Among other things. Did you know that Patrella lived there, and that the whole block of flats had been bought by Sir Franklin Marsh?'

'Yes, I know all that.'

'Perhaps you also know who Myra Destry was. Not the woman who lives at Evesham Mansions, but the woman who was murdered.'

'Perhaps I do,' she said gravely. 'Look, Mr. Cross, will you trust me? I can help you a great deal, but you must let me do it in my own way.'

'Why can't you just say what you know?'

'Because if I did, I don't think I should be of much use to you very long.'

Vicky saw the look in her eyes and guessed what she meant. She felt a little cold chill run down her back. 'Do you mean,' she whispered, 'that they'd . . . ?'

She didn't finish the sentence, but the woman who called herself Audrey Smith understood. 'I told you,' she said, 'that Mr. Midnight is quite ruthless!'

'You could have police protection,' said Gordan. 'They'd be only too pleased to give it you, if you could tell them anything that would catch this fellow.'

'I couldn't tell them anything definite. I don't *know* anything definite — yet. All the police protection in the world wouldn't be any use if it was known that I was mixed up in this.'

Gordan made a gesture of impatience. 'I don't understand. Do you know who Mr. Midnight is?'

'No,' she replied instantly. 'No, I don't. I've a suspicion, but that's all.'

'Is it someone who wears an Intaglio ring?' said Vicky.

Audrey Smith went white to the lips. They thought she was going to faint, but she recovered herself.

'An Intaglio ring,' she repeated in a voice that shook, in spite of her efforts to control it. 'An Intaglio ring . . . how — how did you know about *that*?'

Before they could answer her, she got up quickly and almost ran out of the restaurant.

★ ★ ★

'Interestin' an' peculiar,' grunted Mr. Budd. 'I wonder how this woman came to be mixed up in it.'

He was sitting in the largest easy chair that Gordan's flat boasted, and even this was not big enough for his bulk. He looked as though he had been wedged in by force and would find it very difficult to get himself out again. Gordan and Vicky had just finished telling him about the mysterious Audrey Smith.

'I don't suppose,' he continued ruminatively, 'that Smith's 'er real name. Pity you couldn't find out more about 'er, Mr. Cross.'

'My remark about the ring frightened her,' said Vicky.

'Yes,' said Gordan, 'she was off like a rabbit. I went after her, but the street was rather crowded and she'd disappeared.'

The big man sighed. 'It's all very puzzlin',' he murmured, shaking his head. 'Very puzzlin' indeed. 'Ow do you account for 'er knowin' that you'd be goin' to Castell's flat?'

'I don't,' said Gordan.

'She must've known,' said Mr. Budd sleepily. 'Otherwise she wouldn't 'ave sent the note there. All very mysterious.'

'The greatest mystery of all is Myra Destry,' remarked Gordan. 'Who was she? What was she going to tell me, and why did she give me an address that wasn't hers?'

'But was the address of another Myra Destry,' said Vicky. 'I can't understand it.'

'You surprise me,' murmured Gordan.

'There's no need to be sarcastic,' retorted his wife. 'I can very often understand things that you can't.'

Gordan was trying to think of a crushing reply to this when the front door bell rang. 'I'll go,' he said, and went out into the tiny hall. When he opened the door, he saw Rodney Mayne on the step.

'I'm sorry to bother you, Mr. Cross,' said the visitor nervously, 'but is there any news of Laddie Castell?'

'Not yet, I'm afraid,' answered Gordan. 'Come in.'

Mayne hesitated, and then rather reluctantly crossed the threshold. 'I don't want to be a trouble,' he muttered.

'That's all right. I'm very glad to see you. In here.' He opened the door of the sitting-room and ushered Mayne in. 'Mr. Mayne,' he announced briefly. 'He came to see if there was any news of Castell.'

'Sit down, Mr. Mayne,' said Vicky.

Rodney Mayne sat down in the chair she indicated. He looked a little disconcerted at the presence of Mr. Budd.

'Anxious for news of Castell, are you?' inquired the big man. 'So am I, an' a lot o' people at Scotland Yard. We're all anxious to know what's become of 'im.'

'Do you think anything serious can have happened to him?' asked Mayne, passing a hand nervously across his mouth.

'Unless there's some reason for 'im stayin' away of his own accord, I should say it was pretty certain,' said Mr. Budd.

'What reason could there be?'

'I dunno,' murmured the sleepy-eyed superintendent. 'Unless he's mixed up in this business. 'Ave you ever 'eard of someone called Mr. Midnight, sir?'

'No,' he answered. 'Who's he?'

'We'd all like to know that,' said Gordan. 'Did you know Myra Destry, Mayne?'

'Yes, of course. She was engaged to Laddie; you know that.'

'How well did you know her?'

'She used to come to The Yellow Orchid quite a lot. Look here, you said this morning that she was murdered.'

'She was,' interjected Mr. Budd. 'She was killed at an empty 'ouse in Barnet last night.'

Rodney Mayne moistened his lips. 'Who — who killed her?'

'You thought it might have been Castell this morning, didn't you?' said Gordan. 'Why did you think that?'

'Well, it was only natural, wasn't it? The police were at his flat and — and you told me Myra had been killed. I thought it might have been Laddie.'

'Why?' asked the big man. 'Was Castell the type o' man likely to go round killin' people?'

'No, but — but he had a very hasty temper and he was very jealous of Myra. I thought there might have been a quarrel.'

'Was there any reason why you thought there might have been a quarrel?' snapped Gordan.

'None in particular.' Mayne looked uneasy and nervous. 'I just thought there might have been.'

'I see,' said Gordan. 'Where did Myra Destry live?' he added suddenly.

'She had a flat somewhere. I don't

know where. I think it was quite close to The Yellow Orchid.'

Gordan looked at Mr. Budd, but the stout man appeared to have fallen asleep. Evesham Mansions was a long way away from The Yellow Orchid. 'What makes you think she lived close to The Yellow Orchid?' he asked.

'I don't know . . . something she said once,' answered Mayne. 'She'd forgotten her bag, or something, and she said she'd just run home and get it. She was only gone a few minutes, so I concluded she couldn't live far away.'

'A very natural conclusion, sir,' murmured Mr. Budd without opening his eyes. 'I should 'ave thought the same. 'Ave you got any friends livin' at Evesham Mansions?'

'Evesham Mansions?' repeated Mayne, and he shook his head.

'There's a woman an' her husband livin' at number eight Evesham Mansions,' continued the big man. 'Their name's Destry. The woman's name is Myra Destry.'

Mayne looked surprised and startled. 'You're not telling me that Myra was

93

married?' he said incredulously.

'No — this couldn't 'ave been the Myra Destry you knew,' said Mr. Budd. 'This woman's dark an' she's still alive. Still, it's queer, ain't it? Particularly as your Myra Destry told Mr. Cross that 'er address was eight Evesham Mansions.'

'I can't understand it,' muttered Mayne. 'Unless Myra was a relation.'

'These Destrys say they've never 'eard of 'er,' said Mr. Budd. 'You know a man called Patrella?'

'Yes, he's a regular customer at The Yellow Orchid.'

''E's got a flat at Evesham Mansions, too. An' I'll tell you somethin' else. The man who owns the block o' flats is Sir Franklin Marsh.'

'He owns The Yellow Orchid too.'

'Yes, I know,' said Mr. Budd, suddenly opening his eyes very wide, a disconcerting trick he had, 'an' it's what I call a queer coincidence.'

'I don't see why it should be,' said Rodney Mayne. 'Sir Franklin owns quite a lot of property.'

'Including that empty house at Barnet

where Myra Destry was murdered,' remarked Gordan quietly.

'Everythin' comes back to The Yellow Orchid,' murmured Mr. Budd. The telephone bell rang shrilly and suddenly. The noise of it startled Mayne, and he gave a nervous jump.

'I'll answer it,' said Gordan, as Vicky half rose. He went over and picked up the receiver. There was a confused buzzing and crackling on the line, and then a low, husky voice that he could scarcely hear came over the wire.

'Mr. Cross — is that Mr. Cross?'

'Speaking,' said Gordan.

'It's Williams; you know, Nosey.' The voice was high and urgent. 'I got ter see yer, Mr. Cross. Can yer meet me ternight?'

'Where?' asked Gordan.

'There's a little beer-'ouse just off Lower Thames Street. The Pewter Pot. Come at eight.'

'All right, I'll be there.'

'Don't tell no one yer comin',' said Williams. 'I — ' He broke off suddenly. 'I got to go. Don't forget — at eight ternight.'

There was a click as he hung up the receiver. Gordan put down his own receiver on its rack slowly. If ever he had heard terror in a man's voice, he had heard it in the voice of Nosey Williams.

8

The Pewter Pot was a small public house standing near the river and mostly frequented by watermen, sailors, and the crews of the big sea-going barges unloading at the net by wharves. It had also a sprinkling of workers from the neighbouring markets. Few other people knew of its existence, for it was half hidden at the end of a narrow street that ran down to the river, and was so ramshackle and inconspicuous that you might pass it by a dozen times without being aware that it was there.

A drizzle of rain was falling when Gordan Cross approached this unsalubrious hostelry, and the streets were deserted. Most of the work in the district was done in the early morning, and few people were to be found after the hour of three in the afternoon.

He wondered as he walked quickly along the shining pavement why Nosey

Williams had chosen this particular place for his appointment. It was not one of his regular haunts. There was no information to interest him to be picked up here. The *habitués* of The Pewter Pot, though rough, were honest and hard-working, and Williams made his unpleasant and precarious living by moving among crooks. And then he remembered the fear in the informer's husky voice. Perhaps that was the reason for his choice of venue. Here he would be unknown and unlikely to be seen by any of his cronies.

A clock was striking eight as Gordan turned into the doorway of the pub, pushed open the inner swing-door, and entered the bar. There was only one. It held a sprinkling of customers, a few lightermen, and an official of the Port of London Authority from the pier nearby; but there was no sign of Williams.

Gordan ordered a pint of beer, lit a cigarette, and propped himself up against the stained counter. It was barely time. Something had probably delayed the little nose.

It was nearly a quarter past eight when

Williams came in. He entered the bar quickly and furtively, his small restless eyes sweeping it in a comprehensive glance. He saw Cross and came over to him.

'Sorry I'm late,' he said in a whisper. 'There was someone followin' me, I think, an' I 'ad ter shake 'im off.'

Gordan bought him a pint of beer, and he swallowed half of it thirstily. His thin face was white, and there was a strained look in his eyes that Gordan had not seen there before.

'What did you want to see me about, Nosey?' he asked.

Williams put down the beer-glass and wiped his mouth with the back of his hand. He gave a quick glance round and edged closer along the bar.

'Yer remember what we was talkin' about the other night in The Blue Feathers?' he whispered.

Gordan nodded.

'I've got somethin' about that that might interest yer,' continued Williams, dropping his voice until it was scarcely audible. 'There's somethin' doin' ternight.'

'What do you mean, something doing?'

'A pay-out.'

'Where?' He had raised his voice slightly in his excitement, and the nose made a quick frantic gesture.

'Sh-s-s!' Nosey whispered. 'Not so loud, Mr. Cross.' He shot a worried glance over his shoulder at the other occupants of the bar.

'There's nobody here likely to be interested.'

'Yer never know. You never know who may be listenin.'

'Never mind being so scared,' said Gordan impatiently. 'Tell me more about this pay-out.'

'It's at twelve ternight — the usual time,' said the nose. 'There's a bungalow on the river near Staines called Dreamland. That's where it's 'appenin.'

'Is Mr. Midnight going to be there?'

''Course 'e'll be there. There couldn't be a pay-out without 'im.' He raised his glass to drink the remainder of his beer, and Gordan saw that his hand was trembling.

'Thanks for the information, Nosey,' he said. 'I thought you didn't want to be mixed up in this mess?'

'I don't,' said Nosey Williams fervently. 'I don't, Mr. Cross, but you've done me one or two good turns in past, an' I knew yer'd be interested.'

Gordan was sceptical. There was something more in it than that, he thought. He'd had to drag the hint about The Yellow Orchid out of Williams that evening at The Blue Feathers in Lambeth, and only by using threats had he succeeded. Now he had suddenly come forward of his own accord and volunteered important information — and he was in a muck-sweat of fear. There was something behind it that Gordan couldn't fathom. For some reason, Williams was suddenly anxious to put one over on the mysterious Mr. Midnight; and although he was terrified at doing it, the urge was greater than his fear. What had happened to bring about this change of attitude?

It was useless trying to find out from Williams what had happened. The little nose had given his information and was anxious to be gone. Gordan, who had left his car in a garage nearby, thinking it wiser and less conspicuous to walk the short remaining distance to The Pewter Pot, offered to drop Williams wherever he wished to go; but the other wouldn't hear of it. They parted outside the pub, and Williams vanished into the rain that was now coming down in torrents.

Gordan retrieved his car and drove slowly back to his flat. Vicky was waiting, full of curiosity, to learn what Nosey Williams had had to say. When Gordan told her, the curiosity was replaced by excitement.

'We're going, aren't we?' she exclaimed. 'We're going to this bungalow.'

'*I'm* going,' he corrected her.

'You're not going without me,' she declared.

'Now look here, Vicky. I can't take you.'

'If you don't, I shall go on my own!'

'But don't you see, Vicky — it's dangerous!'

'I don't care. You're not going to leave me out of it. That's what you always want to do when there's any excitement.'

'Excitement!' he echoed. 'There's no knowing what this might develop into. I should feel much happier if you'd keep out of it.'

'Then I'm afraid you're going to be miserable,' said his wife, a light of determination in her eyes. 'I'm coming, and there's nothing you can say that will prevent me.'

Gordan shrugged his shoulders. He knew from past experience that no amount of argument would have any effect. If Vicky had made up her mind, nothing he could say would alter it. If he didn't let her come with him, she would go on her own; and taking her with him was the lesser of two evils.

The rain was sheeting down when they left the flat and headed for Staines. Gordan had decided that it would be better to approach the bungalow from the river, and had telephoned a friend of his who kept a boat-yard near Staines, and arranged to hire a small motor-launch. It was nearly eleven when they drove up to the boatyard, and Reggie Bingham was waiting for them.

'Nice night you've chosen for a river trip,' he remarked. 'I thought you were mad when you telephoned, but I suppose you know what you're doing.'

Gordan grinned. 'This isn't a pleasure trip,' he said.

'I guessed that. What's the idea?'

Gordan explained briefly, and Bingham's eyes sparkled. 'You wouldn't like any help, I suppose?' he suggested rather wistfully. 'It might be useful if I came along a looked after the boat.'

'I'd be glad if you would,' said Gordan, to his evident delight, 'but I ought to warn you that there may be trouble — bad trouble.'

'That suits me,' Bingham said. 'I'm all for a bit of excitement.'

'You might get more than you bargained for before the night's over. The man I'm hoping to find is dangerous. By the way, do you know a place called Dreamland?'

'Yes, it's a bungalow not very far from here. I thought it was empty.'

'It won't be empty tonight,' answered Gordan, grinning. 'Come on; we'd better be going.'

They made their way down the landing-stage to where a little launch was rocking gently at her moorings. Bingham stripped off the waterproof covering and helped Vicky into the boat. He started the engine, switched on the navigation lights, and when Gordan had joined them in the boat, untied the painter and cast off. The little boat swung away from the landing-stage, and Bingham made a wide sweep, turning the prow downstream.

'Can you shut the lights off when we get to the bungalow?' asked Gordan, peering ahead through the curtain of rain.

Bingham nodded. 'I hope there isn't a Conservancy boat about,' he said. 'I shouldn't think there's likely to be on a night like this. What do we do when we get to the bungalow?'

'Cruise slowly past and see if there's any sign of life. Then we'll turn and drift into the bank as near to the place as possible. The important thing is that we shouldn't be spotted.'

'Leave it to me.'

The little launch chugged slowly downstream. With the rain falling like a veil in front of the dim navigation lights, it was very difficult to see. There was a chill wind, and this and the damp made Vicky shiver. She was wearing a mackintosh, but it offered little protection from such a downpour, and there was no cover in the open launch.

Presently, Bingham stopped the engine and let the boat drift with the stream. 'The bungalow should be somewhere just here,' he muttered, peering towards the left-hand bank.

'I can't see anything,' said Vicky.

Bingham reached forward and switched off the lights. 'That better?' he said.

'Yes, a little.' She could see now the shadowy bank of the river and the vague bulk of trees. There were a few houses of the bungalow type grouped fairly close together, with gardens that ran down to the water's edge.

'Surely Dreamland isn't one of these?' said Gordan.

'No,' replied Bingham. 'If I remember rightly, it stands more or less by itself. It's a fairly large place. Just round this bend, I think.' He steered the little boat round a sudden bend in the river and brought it in nearer the bank. 'There you are,' he said.

'That's the place you want.'

They made out the dim shape of a white building, low-built and lying well back from the water's edge. There was no sign of life about it. The windows were dark and shuttered, and nothing stirred. If Mr. Midnight had chosen this place for one of his periodical pay-outs for the stolen property he bought, thought Gordan as he eyed it, he could scarcely have found a better spot. It was silent, deserted and ideal for the purpose. Any number of people could meet here at night, and no one would be the wiser.

'There's a piece of waste ground close to the place,' whispered Reggie Bingham. 'Shall I take her in there?'

Gordan nodded, and the little launch edged silently into the dark bank. Presently there was a barely perceptible bump, and Bingham reached over the side and held or a bush. 'What do we do now?' he inquired.

'I think we'll land and explore,' said Gordan. He jumped up on to the bank. 'Give me the painter, Vicky,' he whispered, 'and I'll make it fast.'

She threw it up to him. He found the root of a tree and tied the boat up to it securely. Bingham joined him, and they turned and helped Vicky up beside them.

'Now,' whispered Gordan, 'let's have a look at the bungalow — and for the Lord's sake, don't make any noise.'

They moved off stealthily towards a low fence that divided the garden of the bungalow from the waste ground. There was no sound except the hiss of the falling rain and the lapping of the river against the bank.

The fence was quite low, and they experienced little difficulty in climbing it. They tried to persuade Vicky to stay where she was, but she refused, and it was impossible argue with her. They stood in the neglected garden, listening. Everything was quite still. From the bungalow, which loomed beside them, there was no sound at all.

'There doesn't appear to be anyone here,' whispered Bingham after a pause.

'Don't be too sure,' answered Gordan. 'They wouldn't be likely to advertise their presence.'

'But surely we should see some glimmer of light,' said Vicky. 'I think the place is deserted.'

'Let's see what it's like from the other side,' said Gordan.

Cautiously they made their way round the side of the building. The back was as dark as the front. No vehicle stood near the little gate, or in the lane that ran past it. They stopped under the shadow of a willow.

'There's nobody here,' whispered Bingham, and his voice was tinged with disappointment. As he finished speaking, a clock in the distance began to strike twelve. The measured strikes came faintly through the damp air. This was the time when Mr. Midnight should have been here — the time he always chose to transact his business with his dubious associates and which had earned him his curious name. Had Nosey Williams's information been wrong, or had something happened to warn Mr. Midnight off?

'Listen!' breathed Vicky, suddenly clutching Gordan's arm.

They all heard it — the sound of oars

from the river. It might not be anything, but it was unlikely that any ordinary person would be out on the river at that time on such a night. Almost holding their breath, they listened with straining ears. The sound of the oars drew nearer and then ceased. The rower was letting his boat drift. After a lapse of time that seemed an eternity, but could not have been more than a few minutes, they heard a gentle bump. The boat had touched the camp-shedding at the foot of the garden. There was the scrape of a foot on concrete, and the rattle of an iron ring. Somebody had tied the boat up and had landed. They heard the swish of someone forcing their way through the weeds, and then — dead silence. Whoever the person was, he had stopped. Gordan could picture him standing and staring at the dark bungalow from the middle of the garden.

'Come on,' he whispered so softly that Vicky and Bingham scarcely heard him. 'I'm going to see who it is.'

He moved cautiously away, round the side of the bungalow, the other two behind him. It was very dark, and he could scarcely make out the darker shape which marked the whereabouts of the midnight visitor. He was standing motionless, as Gordan had visualized, facing the house.

Gordan felt in the pocket of his raincoat, and his fingers closed over the torch he had brought with him. He drew it out noiselessly, pointed it in the direction of silent watcher, and pressed the button. A blinding ray of light focused on the man who stood there.

He gave a startled cry of alarm and turned to run, but Gordan had seen his face and recognized him.

It was Richard Destry!

Reggie Bingham caught him as he was trying to scramble back into the dinghy. 'Oh no, you don't!' he cried, gripping Destry by the collar and hauling him back onto the landing-stage.

'Let me go!' panted the man. 'What do you think you're doing? Who are you?'

'I think you know me, Mr. Destry,' said Gordan.

'How should I know you?' snarled Destry, struggling to free himself from Bingham's grip. 'What the devil do you mean by attacking me?'

'I think you remember me,' interrupted Gordan. 'I called at your flat to inquire about Myra Destry.'

Destry stopped struggling. He was still a little breathless, but his voice had lost the note of panic when spoke. 'Oh, that's who you are, is it?' he said, and he sounded both surprised and relieved. 'What the dickens are you doing here?'

'I'd like to know what *you're* doing here,' retorted Gordan.

'I don't see that that's any business of yours. Let me tell you that you're on private property.'

'So are you, for that matter.'

'I'm entitled to be here,' replied the other curtly. 'This happens to be my bungalow.'

'I thought you lived at Evesham Mansions.'

'So I do. But I rent this place.'

'Oh, you do, do you?' said Cross. 'What brought you here tonight?'

Destry tried to jerk himself free from Bingham, but the boat-yard owner held him too firmly. 'Let me go!' he snarled angrily. 'This is outrageous!'

'I'm not letting you go until Cross says so,' answered Reggie Bingham cheerfully.

'You'll get in trouble for this,' cried Destry. 'All of you.'

'I doubt it,' said Gordan. 'You're the one who's likely to get the trouble. What are you doing here?'

'Can't a man visit his own property? You've no right to — '

'Rather a funny time to choose, isn't it?' interrupted Gordan. 'Twelve o'clock on a rainy night.'

'Is that any concern of yours? I can come here when I like.'

'That depends what you came *for*. Were you expecting to meet someone here?'

'Who should I be expecting to meet?'

'A gentleman called Mr. Midnight.'

'Look here, are you mad?' said Destry. 'I don't know anyone with such a ridiculous name. It sounds like something out of a book.'

'It applies to a very real person,' said Gordan. 'And a very dangerous person, too. Myra Destry found that out!'

'I don't know what you're talking

about. Myra is my wife, and I can assure you that she knows nothing about anyone called Mr. Midnight.'

'I'm not referring to that Myra Destry. I mean the woman who was murdered.'

There was a dull explosion, and something buzzed viciously past his ear. The shot was almost instantly followed by a second and a third.

'Down!' snapped Gordan quickly, and he pulled Vicky down among the dripping weeds.

Three more shots came in rapid succession. Gordan saw the thin pencil of flame from the barrel of the automatic thrust through one of the windows of the bungalow, and heard the smack of the bullets as they hit the sodden ground near him. He waited, pressing Vicky down close to him, for further shots, but none came. There was complete silence once more, except for the hiss and patter of the falling rain. He allowed a long interval to elapse after the last shot, and then he cautiously raised himself.

'Better look out,' whispered Bingham. 'He may be still there.'

Gordan raised his arm and flashed on the torch. But there was no answering shot. 'I think he's gone,' he muttered.

'Who was it?' quavered Destry. All his previous belligerency had vanished. He was a badly scared and frightened man.

'You know very well who it was,' snapped Gordan. 'Have you got a key to the place?'

'Yes — yes, of course I've got a key,' answered Destry. 'I don't know what you mean. How should I know who did the shooting?'

'Because he was shooting at you!' retorted Gordan.

Destry uttered a little gasp of terror. 'I don't believe it,' he stammered. 'You're trying to scare me!'

'I don't have to scare you. You're frightened out of your wits as it is. Come along; I'm going to see inside that bungalow.'

'For heaven's sake, be careful, darling,' said Vicky.

'I'm not going with you,' broke in Destry.

'You came to see your property, and

you're going to,' said Gordan. 'You stay here, Vicky — or better still, go back to the launch.'

'I'm coming with you,' she declared.

'You're not,' said Gordan firmly. 'For once I want you to listen to me and stay out of danger.'

The silence was broken by the sudden chug-chug of a motor-engine. 'That's the launch!' cried Bingham. 'Somebody's started it up.'

'Our friend with the gun,' said Gordan grimly, 'making his getaway!'

The noise of the little engine grew louder. Peering through the rainy darkness, they saw the black smudge of the boat as it shot out into midstream. A dim unrecognizable figure was crouched over the wheel.

'We ought to have stopped him,' muttered Bingham as the sound of the engine grew fainter.

'I think we were wiser not to attempt it,' said Gordan. 'It's not much use arguing with a gun!'

'How are we going to get back?' said Vicky.

'We shall have to walk,' answered her

husband, 'unless we use the boat Destry came in.'

'There isn't room,' said Destry quickly. 'It's only a small one.'

'How far did you come in it?' asked Bingham curiously.

'Never mind that now,' interrupted Gordan. 'I want to see the inside of this bungalow.'

He led the way over to the door. It was set between two long windows and under the shadow of a jutting balcony.

'Key,' said Gordan laconically, holding out his hand to Destry.

The man hesitated. Then, reluctantly, he put his hand in the pocket of his raincoat and produced a key. 'There you are,' he grunted ungraciously.

Gordan took the key and thrust it into the lock. It turned easily, and he pushed open the door. It was pitch dark within the small hall until he switched on his torch sent the ray darting from left to right.

The hall was comfortably furnished. There was a thick carpet on the floor; the reddish copper of a warming-pan caught the light and reflected it back; a rather

117

fine oak chest stood against one wall. But there was a close, musty smell — the smell of a building that had been shut up for some time.

There were two doors opening off the hall, one on either side. Gordan chose the one on the left, turned the handle, and threw it open. The room beyond was furnished as a living-room. It was quite large, and there was another door set in the wall facing the window. He opened this and discovered a kitchen — a tiny place, but well fitted. On the floor of the living-room he found the ejected shells from an automatic. It was from here that the shooter had fired. In further support of this, the carpet was covered with muddy footprints, the marks apparently of a rather large foot.

There was nothing else of interest, and he turned his attention to the other room across the hall. The door here was locked.

'Have you got the key to this?' asked Gordan, turning to Richard Destry.

Destry shook his head. 'It should be in the lock.'

It wasn't. Gordan took the key out of

the other door, but it didn't fit. If Destry was speaking the truth, somebody had locked the door and taken away the key.

'I'm going to have a look in that room,' said Gordan, and, stepping back, he flung himself heavily against the door. It withstood the first attack, but at the second there was a splintering of wood, and it flew open.

This room was a bedroom. A large double divan bed occupied most of the space, but in front of the window there was a kidney-shaped dressing-table draped with the same damask as the buttoned bed-head.

It was a woman's room. The glass top of the dressing-table was covered with perfume bottles and lotions; there was a huge cut-glass powder bowl with a puff lying beside it. The air was heavy with perfume.

Gordan recognized that scent immediately. It had come wafting across his nostrils when the woman who called herself Myra Destry had leaned over him in The Yellow Orchid.

9

Vicky confirmed his opinion. 'It's the same perfume,' she said. She went over to the dressing-table and touched the top of a flask. 'Here you are — Le numero cinq — Molyneux. She had nice taste in perfume, poor woman.'

'See if the lights work,' said Gordan, and she went over to the door and pressed down the switch. Shaded wall-brackets came on, shedding a soft rose-coloured glow over the dainty room.

'Look here,' said Destry. 'I don't understand this. This bungalow is mine. The only person who's occupied this room is my wife.'

'Does she use this perfume?' asked Gordan.

Destry shook his head. His face was puzzled. 'No,' he answered.

'How long is it since you've been here?'

'Several months. I don't know exactly when we were here last. Sometime back in the summer.'

'It's been occupied recently.' Gordan ran his fingers over the top of the dressing-table. There was only the thinnest film of dust. 'What's through that door there?' He nodded towards a door facing the window.

'The bathroom,' said Destry.

Gordan went over and opened the door. It was well-appointed, with a shower, the glass shelves laden with expensive bath salts and toilet preparations. Here again there were signs of recent occupation. The sponge was still damp; a tube of toothpaste with the screw top off had not dried.

'You see,' said Gordan, pointing these out, 'somebody's been here within the last few days.'

Destry frowned. 'I can assure you it was neither myself nor my wife. We haven't been here for months.'

'What made you suddenly decide to come here tonight?'

'My wife asked me to collect some things she left here in the summer.' The answer came quickly enough, but there was an expression in the man's eyes that told Gordan he was lying.

'It was rather a peculiar time to choose, wasn't it?'

Destry shrugged his shoulders. 'I suppose it was. I'd been spending the evening with some friends who live near here, and I thought it a good opportunity.'

'Is that where you got the boat from?'

'Yes.'

Gordan did not believe a word of it, but there was nothing he could do. If the bungalow was his property, he was entitled to visit it when he liked, without offering any explanation. The fact that there had been an unauthorized person lurking in the place could not be proved to have anything to do with Destry. They might have surprised an armed burglar, though Gordan, thought it was very unlikely. The law would undoubtedly support Destry if he liked to make a fuss about their presence at the bungalow.

The man appeared to sense what was passing in Gordan's mind, for he smiled a little sneeringly as he said: 'Any more questions?'

'Not at the moment,' answered Gordan. 'Maybe the police will want to ask you some later.'

'The police?'

'The presence of this person with a gun will have to be reported. So will the fact that this place has been occupied by someone without your knowledge.'

Destry looked a trifle uneasy. 'I don't want to be involved in a lot of trouble,' he said. 'It doesn't look as if there's been any damage done.'

'It's not a question of damage. Unless I'm mistaken, this place was occupied by a woman who was murdered, and the police will want to know all about it.'

'I don't know anything about this woman you keep on talking about. Who was she? When was she murdered?'

'She called herself Myra Destry, and she was killed at an empty house in Barnet last night,' said Gordan curtly.

'Is that the woman you were looking for when you called at my flat this morning?'

'Yes.' Gordan looked at him steadily. 'She gave me your address and said she lived there.'

'That was obviously a lie.'

'Possibly; but the whole thing is very queer.'

'I know nothing about this woman — nothing at all,' insisted Destry. 'What made her give you my address?'

'I should like to be able to answer that. I should also like to know why she called herself Myra Destry.'

Gordan obtained grudging permission from Destry to search the bungalow. The big wardrobe was full of dresses — expensive gowns and suits, bearing the name of a well-known West End fashion house. There were several pairs of shoes, all equally expensive, and in the chest of drawers a number of sets of underwear and other items of feminine apparel. Destry swore that none of these things belonged to his wife.

Hidden under a drawer full of stockings, Gordan discovered a small black leather book. It was full of pencilled notes — addresses, and what appeared to be telephone numbers. On the fly-leaf had been scrawled the name 'Myra Destry'. Gordan put the little book in his pocket for perusal later. There was not much doubt that the murdered woman had been living here, though why she should have taken up her abode in a bungalow that didn't belong to her was a mystery. Everything about her was a mystery, including the reason for her assumption of a name that apparently was not her own.

There was nothing else of any interest in the bungalow. Before they left, Destry unlocked a small writing desk in the living-room and took out a large heavily sealed envelope which, he said, was what he had come there to fetch. He explained that it contained documents relating to some property belonging to his wife, but whether this was the truth or not, Gordan had no means of judging.

They came out of the bungalow to find that the rain had abated slightly. Gordan locked the door and returned the key to Destry. 'The police will want it,' he said. 'There's no doubt that they'll want to make a thorough inspection of the place.'

Destry hesitated. 'You'd better keep it,' he said after a moment's thought. 'I don't want them bothering me.'

'They'll bother you in any case. This bungalow is your property, and they'll certainly want to question you about the woman who's been living here.'

'But I don't know anything about her. I've told you that.'

'Tell the police that,' said Gordan. 'Perhaps the believe you, and perhaps they won't.'

He made his way through the weed-choked garden to the waterfront. The dinghy was rocking gently, bumping softly against the landing-stage.

'It's going to be a tight squeeze to get the four of us in that,' remarked Bingham, peering down at the little boat, 'particularly with all that stuff you've got in the bottom.'

'Stuff — what stuff?' demanded Destry. 'There's nothing in the boat.'

'What's that then?' said Bingham. He leaned down to look closer and they heard his quick gasp. 'Turn your light on here, Cross,' he cried. 'There's a man in the boat.'

Gordan flashed the torch down on to

the floor of the dinghy. A man lay huddled in the bottom of the boat, his white face queerly streaked with brown.

It was Laddie Castell! He was quite dead, and the brown substance streaked across his face was dried blood!

★   ★   ★

The dark, wet garden of the bungalow was lit briefly and vividly by the light of the photographer's flash bulb. The dazzling glare brought out every detail with startling clearness for the fraction of a second, and then darkness enveloped everything once more, like a thick blanket. Again and again, the flashes made tree and shrub and the white facade of the building leap out, silhouetting in dense black the group of men who stood by the little boat, still rocking gently at its mooring.

Gordan Cross had telephoned to Mr. Budd after the finding of Laddie Castell's body. The telephone in the bungalow was still connected, and he had no difficulty in getting through. He had aroused the big man from his bed, but his news had quickly brought him to full wakefulness. In an incredibly short space of time, a big police car had sped to a stop in front of the bungalow, disgorging Mr. Budd, a police photographer, the local inspector, and a very weary and unhappy-looking Leek. The police surgeon followed in his own car a few minutes later.

Mr. Budd had listened in silence, stifling a battery of yawns, while Gordan had briefly given an account of the events of the night, culminating with the discovery of Castell's body in the bottom of the dinghy. Still without comment, the superintendent issued swift orders, and all the routine of a police investigation got quickly underway.

When the photographs had been taken, the body was lifted out of the boat and carried into the bungalow. It was laid on the table in the kitchen, and the doctor made his examination.

Castell had been shot. The bullet had struck him squarely between the eyes, and it had been fired at close range, for there were powder burns on the forehead. It had passed clean through the brain and made its exit by a ragged wound at the back of the head. Death, said the police surgeon, must have been instantaneous.

'The question is,' said Mr. Budd when these preliminaries had been completed, ''ow did he get in that boat?'

'Better ask Destry,' said Gordan.

'I know nothing about it,' the man insisted. 'There was nothing in the boat when I tied it up — I swear there wasn't.'

'Did you know this man, Castell?' asked Mr. Budd, surveying him sleepily.

Destry shook his head. 'No. I've never seen him before in my life.'

'Who was this feller who was in the bungalow? The feller what did the shootin'?'

'I don't know that, either. The whole thing's a complete mystery to me.'

'It's a mystery to me, too,' said Mr. Budd. 'But it ain't goin' to remain one.' He looked about him through eyes that were almost completely closed. 'This is your bungalow?'

'I rented it, but I haven't been here for a long time.'

'You rented it, eh? Who did you rent it from?'

There was a momentary hesitation before Destry replied, 'Sir Franklin Marsh.'

Budd's eyes opened suddenly. He looked very wide awake and alert. 'That's interestin',' he murmured. 'Very interestin'. Sir Franklin Marsh, eh? It's surprisin' how that feller keeps croppin' up in this business.'

'What do you mean?' asked Destry. He tried to infuse surprise in his voice, but Gordan thought it was badly done. Destry knew very well what the big man meant.

'Sir Franklin Marsh owns a place called The Yellow Orchid where this feller, Castell, was band leader,' said Mr. Budd thoughtfully. ''E also owns that empty 'ouse at Barnet where the woman who called 'erself Myra Destry was murdered. 'E's recently bought that block o' flats, Evesham Mansions, where you live and where the murdered woman *said* she lived, an' now we find 'e owns this place, where it's pretty certain she *did* live.'

'I'm sure he didn't know anything about that,' Destry put in quickly.

'I don't know how you can be sure o' that.'

'This place belongs to me. I pay Sir Franklin a rent for it. Is it likely he would allow anybody else to live in it?'

'You mean this woman was livin' 'ere without permission from anyone?'

'Yes — if she *did* live here.'

'I don't think there's much doubt about that,' remarked Gordan. 'All those clothes and things — you say they don't belong to your wife?'

Destry made a gesture of helplessness. 'That's true. I don't understand it. It seems incredible that she should have calmly taken possession of somebody else's property like that. How did she know that we might not turn up suddenly?'

'Ah, yes,' murmured Mr. Budd softly. 'I'm very glad you've raised that point, Mr. Destry. 'Ow *did* she know that?'

'Perhaps you can suggest an answer. I can't.'

'P'raps I could.' Mr. Budd gently rubbed his chin. 'Yes, maybe I could, if I tried very hard. Maybe it's 'ad somethin' to do with 'er callin' 'erself Myra Destry.'

'There may be some explanation for that in the notebook I found,' suggested Gordan. He took it out of his pocket. 'It obviously belonged to the dead woman.'

They cleared a small table in the living-room and, under the light of a lamp, he and Mr. Budd examined the little book together. It was quite small — one of those limp leather notebooks that can be bought at any good stationer's. It was not a diary — the pages were ruled in faint blue lines, but were not dated. The first entry seemed to be some kind of a shopping list. The writing was difficult to make out, but Gordan could decipher something about 'eggs' and a word that was definitely 'soap-flakes'. The next entry was an appointment: 'L. 12.30. Maroc's.' The L. probably referred to Laddie. Maroc's was a well-known West End restaurant. This was followed by several telephone numbers.

'We'll check up on these,' murmured Mr. Budd. 'Maybe they'll supply us with some useful information. Hello, what's this?'

He pointed with a stubby finger to the

next entry. It consisted of a list of names, headed by Sir Franklin Marsh. The complete list ran:

Sir Franklin Marsh
Patrella
Macbane
Destry

A big question mark had been scrawled beside the list, and on the opposite page was written: 'The man had a ring — an Intaglio ring. Does this mean anything?' A few pages further on, there was a rough sketch of some building, but what it was supposed to represent neither Mr. Budd nor Gordan could make out. The last entry was the most important. 'Whose face was behind the mask? Who was the woman? She wasn't with them; she was watching.'

'Whose face was behind the mask?' repeated Gordan softly. 'What did she mean by that?'

Mr. Budd pulled gently at his large nose. 'I think she saw one o' these periodical pay-outs of Mr. Midnight's. 'Is was the face behind the mask.' He peered again at the scrawled entry. 'Who was the woman?' he said speculatively.

'That's an easy one,' answered Gordan. 'I think the woman who was watching was the one who calls herself 'A. Smith'.'

10

It was a weary little party that sat drinking hot coffee in the sitting-room of Gordan Cross's flat a few hours later. Mr. Budd, his big face pale with fatigue, was wedged in the biggest easy chair. Leek, looking the picture of misery, blinked sleepily at the cup in his hand and wondered how long it would be before he could go back to his interrupted slumbers. Vicky, openly yawning, had curled herself up in a corner of the settee, the coffee-pot on a small table near her, hoping that they would soon go and she could get to bed. Gordan seemed to be the only one the events of the night had left with any energy. He was pacing up and down, a cigarette between his lips, frowning thoughtfully.

Outside, the dawn was just breaking — a grey, cold and unpleasant morning. The rain had ceased, but the heavy clouds that were driving across the sky before a stiff wind looked sullen and ominous. There would be more rain if the wind dropped. Gordan stopped by the window and peered out at the uninviting prospect. There was something depressing about the general greyness, or perhaps it was his own tiredness and feeling of frustration that made it seem so.

The night had been a busy one, but they had got very little further towards discovering the identity of the mysterious Mr. Midnight. The unknown person who had shot at them from the bungalow might have been he, but there was no proof. And even if there had been, they were still unaware who it was. The launch in which he had made his escape had been found by a lock-keeper drifting down the river, abandoned and empty. There was little doubt that it was from this launch that the body of Castell had been transferred to the dinghy. The transfer must have taken place while they were all inside the bungalow, unless Destry had been lying and *he* had brought the man's body with him.

Both Gordan and Mr. Budd considered

this to be unlikely, but as a precaution, the superintendent had arranged for Destry to be kept under observation. Just why Castell's body had been brought to the bungalow at all, or, if it had been there all the time, why it had been put in the boat, was something none of them could fathom. It was merely one more mystery to add to the total that was steadily piling up.

According to Nosey Williams, the bungalow had been chosen as the venue for one of Mr. Midnight's periodical pay-outs, but for some reason or other, this must have been cancelled. Certainly no one besides the mysterious shooter and Destry had put in an appearance there. What had happened to make necessary this sudden alteration in Mr. Midnight's plans? Or had the little nose been misinformed? His information was usually reliable — he had built up his unsavoury reputation on his reliability. Had he slipped up this time, or had he been deliberately misinformed by someone who knew that he would pass the information on? Was that it?

Gordan had concluded that the shooter had been after Destry — but had he? Had he been waiting in the bungalow for *them*? Had the whole thing been engineered with the object of decoying them to the bungalow, where the gunman would be waiting? If that were the case, how did Destry fit in? Had he been sent to see that the orders had been carried out, or had his arrival been unexpected?

'I can't make up my mind about this business,' he said aloud, stubbing out his cigarette in an ashtray.

'What's the use of trying at this hour of the morning?' said Vicky, yawning. 'Why can't we go to bed?'

'That's a very good idea, Mrs. Cross,' remarked Mr. Budd, opening his eyes; and Sergeant Leek visibly brightened at the suggestion. 'We're all pretty tired, an' there's nothin' much more we can do for a bit.'

'What's the next move?' asked Gordan. 'What are you going to do?'

'I'm goin' home ter get a few hours' sleep,' said the big man, getting out of the chair with difficulty.

'I mean after that,' interrupted Gordan impatiently.

Mr. Budd yawned widely and long. 'I think I shall pay a visit to this feller Sir Franklin Marsh. That seems to me to be a pretty good idea.'

'I was going to suggest the same thing,' said Gordan. 'Do you mind if I come with you?'

Mr. Budd considered this, rubbing his chin. 'I don't see why not,' he answered after a pause. 'Maybe it's a good idea.'

'I'll meet you at the Yard at eleven. Marsh lives in Chelsea, doesn't he?'

'Got a big 'ouse on Cheyney Walk,' said Mr. Budd, nodding his head slowly. 'Bought it about a year ago.'

'The way that man collects property is remarkable.'

'an' three years ago 'e was broke an' owed money all over the place,' murmured Mr. Budd. 'As you say, Mr. Cross, it's remarkable. It'd be interestin' to know where the money came from, wouldn't it?'

★ ★ ★

Sir Franklin Marsh was in bed when they arrived at the house on Cheyney Walk. A flabby-faced manservant informed them of this fact in a tone of great satisfaction, adding that his master had given him strict instructions that he was on no account to be disturbed.

'I'm afraid 'e'll 'ave to be,' said Mr. Budd, producing his card and giving it to the man. 'Take this up to 'im an' say that we wish to see 'im for a few minutes, an' that the matter's urgent.' The manservant glanced at the card and his face changed. The supercilious look was replaced by an expression of apprehension. He ushered them into the hall and disappeared up the wide staircase.

Gordan looked round appraisingly. The place was beautifully furnished. The carpets and fittings were the most expensive kind obtainable, and in the best possible taste. There was no lack of money here. And three years ago, Sir Franklin Marsh had been broke. Where had the money come from?

The flabby-faced manservant reappeared. His attitude had altered completely. 'Sir

140

Franklin will see you, sir,' he said almost obsequiously. 'Come this way, if you please.' He led the way up the stairs and opened the door of a room on the first landing. 'If you'll wait in here, Sir Franklin will be with you in a few minutes.' He bowed and left them, shutting the door behind him.

The room was fitted as a study. Book-shelves, breast-high, surrounded the panelled walls. A huge antique writing table was set across one corner, and a group of deep and comfortable-looking easy chairs faced the fireplace. The carpet was so thick it was like walking on a well-kept lawn, and the few pictures were by the most famous and expensive of the moderns.

'Does 'imself well, eh?' murmured Mr. Budd.

Gordan nodded. 'How does he manage it?'

The big man shrugged his massive shoulders. 'There's quite a lot o' ways of makin' money these days, if you ain't too partic'lar. That place of 'is, The Yellow Orchid, must be bringin' in a tidy bit.'

'But he had to have money in the first place. You can't open a venue like The

Yellow Orchid without it.'

'Maybe someone left 'im a fortune,' said Mr. Budd. 'Or maybe 'e's buyin' things cheap an' sellin' 'em dear. There's a lot o' money ter be made that way — if you can get in the right market.'

'Particularly if the things you buy happen to be stolen.'

Mr. Budd shook his head chidingly. 'You mustn't go sayin' things like that, Mr. Cross. You'll be gettin' in trouble. There's a law o' slander, yer know.'

The door opened suddenly, and Sir Franklin Marsh came in. He was wearing a silk dressing-gown over pyjamas, and Gordan thought he looked very tired.

He looked quickly from one to the other. 'I'm sorry to have kept you waiting,' he said, addressing Mr. Budd, 'but I had a very late night last night. What is it you want to see me about?'

'I understand, sir,' said Mr. Budd slowly, 'that you own a bungalow on the river near Staines called Dreamland?'

'That's correct. What about it?'

Mr. Budd told him briefly what had happened on the previous night.

142

'Good heavens!' exclaimed the grey-haired man when he had finished. 'It's incredible — but I can't quite see what it has to do with me. I let the place some time ago.'

'To a man called Richard Destry?' asked Mr. Budd.

'Yes, that's right.'

'I believe you knew Myra Destry, the woman who was murdered?' put in Gordan.

'I knew her slightly.' Sir Franklin helped himself to a cigarette from a box on the desk and lit it carefully. 'She used to come to The Yellow Orchid quite frequently. I believe she was engaged to Castell.'

'What do you know about her?' said Mr. Budd.

Sir Franklin Marsh blew out a little stream of smoke, and examined the end of his cigarette with great deliberation. 'Very little. No more than I know about a good many of the people who come to The Yellow Orchid. She was a very pleasant woman. Surely the person who could tell you all about her would be this man Destry.'

'He says he knows nothing about her,'

said the big man. 'They weren't related.'

'But her name was the same, and you tell me she was living at the bungalow,' said Sir Franklin quickly. 'Surely.'

'Destry insists that he was unaware that she was living there,' said Gordan. 'He says that she was quite unknown to him.'

Sir Franklin Marsh raised his eyebrows. 'Didn't I see you at The Yellow Orchid the other night?' he inquired abruptly.

'You did. There was a little argument about a table with one of your patrons, a man called Patrella.'

'Ah, yes, I remember. Quite a lot of fuss about nothing. Patrella's like that — a nice fellow, but fussy.' He changed the conversation again abruptly. 'You know your own business best, but don't you think it rather a queer coincidence that both these people should have the same name Destry and not know each other?'

'A very queer coincidence,' said Gordan. 'I'll tell you a queerer one — Richard Destry's wife's name is Myra Destry, too.'

Sir Franklin regarded him steadily. 'That's a most extraordinary coincidence, as you say,' he remarked evenly. 'I should be rather inclined to doubt such a coincidence myself.'

'We're not entirely satisfied about it, sir,' said Mr. Budd. 'We were 'opin' that you might be able to help us.'

'My dear — er — ' Sir Franklin glanced at the card he had put down on the desk. 'My dear Superintendent, I know nothing about these people — nothing at all. How should I?'

'Mr. Destry and his wife occupy a flat in Evesham Mansions,' said Mr. Budd. 'I believe that's your property as well, sir.'

'Your belief is correct,' said Sir Franklin, 'but I'm not personally acquainted with the history of all my tenants. My agent attends to the letting of the flats.'

'Did he attend to the letting of the bungalow?' asked Gordan.

'Certainly.'

'But you knew it had been let to a man called Destry?'

'There's nothing very remarkable in that. When the offer was made, my agent naturally referred the matter to me. I left all the negotiations in his hands, but when you mentioned the name Destry, I remembered.'

'You didn't associate Myra Destry with the person who had rented the bungalow?' asked Gordan.

'If I did, I probably thought they were related. As I told you, I didn't know Miss Destry very well. I spoke to her once or twice when she came to The Yellow Orchid, that's all.'

It was all very plausible. There was not even the flicker of uneasiness about Sir Franklin Marsh's manner, but Gordan felt that there was something wrong somewhere. This man had denied being in the Lambeth pub on the night he, Gordan, had met Nosey Williams there; but the reporter was quite certain it had been he, and equally convinced that his presence had scared Williams pretty considerably.

'You own the house at Barnet in which Myra Destry was murdered?' he said, and it was more a statement than a question.

'Yes,' replied Sir Franklin, 'I own a considerable amount of property.'

'All acquired within the last three years?'

For the first time, he saw a ripple of disquiet pass over the face of the other. It barely disturbed the surface, and it was gone in an instant; but it had shown for a moment, and Gordan knew that the man was uneasy.

'Yes, I think it was during that period.' Sir Franklin stubbed out the butt of his cigarette in the ashtray with great care.

'I understand, sir,' said Mr. Budd, and his tone was apologetic, 'that up to that time you were not very well off?'

Sir Franklin Marsh turned from the ashtray and eyed him coldly. 'I fail to see how that's any business of yours, Superintendent.'

'The fact's pretty well known, sir,' murmured the big man.

'That may or may not be correct,' said Sir Franklin in a voice that was brittle as glass. 'Whether it is or not is entirely my concern. You have no right whatever to question me about my private affairs, and I refuse to discuss them.'

He was within his rights, and Mr. Budd knew it. He mumbled an apology and cleared his throat. 'You can't give us any information then, sir,' he said, 'about the murdered woman, Myra Destry?'

'I know nothing about any of these people.'

'Perhaps your agents could help. Could you give me the name?'

'Bulmer and Whitton,' answered the grey-haired man without hesitation. 'Their offices are on Hay Hill, off Piccadilly. They might be able to tell you something; I don't know.' His manner had changed abruptly. He was almost genial. 'I'm sorry I can't be of more assistance. I'm very sorry about this poor woman. It was a dreadful thing to happen. So many dreadful things happen these days. The newspapers are full of them. This man, Mr. Midnight . . . ' He stopped suddenly, trying to cover up his mistake.

''Ow did you come to 'ear of him?' asked Mr. Budd.

'I — I don't know.' Sir Franklin was confused and stammered slightly. 'I read about it somewhere.'

'Not in the newspapers,' said Gordan. 'There's been no mention of Mr. Midnight in the newspapers — yet.'

'I've heard the name somewhere,' said Sir Franklin with a gesture of impatience.

'I thought I'd seen it in one of the papers.'

'That's impossible,' said Gordan.

'Well, it was somewhere,' snapped Sir Franklin irritably. 'I couldn't have imagined it!'

'No, sir, you couldn't 'ave imagined it,' remarked Mr. Budd, shaking his head slowly. 'That's what makes it so interestin' an' peculiar.'

11

'I don't think there's any doubt that Sir Franklin Marsh is in this business up to his neck,' said Gordan, and Mr. Budd nodded slowly. They were sitting in a small tea shop on King's Road discussing their recent interview over two steaming cups of coffee.

'I agree with you,' said the big man, helping himself to sugar. 'But there'd be difficulty proving it.'

'Marsh is a clever man, but he made a bad slip when he mentioned Mr. Midnight. Unless he has some inside information, how did he ever hear of him? The general public know nothing about him. I didn't until I heard about him from Nosey Williams.'

'You're right there,' said Mr. Budd. He gulped down some of the hot coffee, burned his tongue, and nearly choked.

'You should be more careful,' admonished Gordan.

Mr. Budd took out his handkerchief and wiped his streaming eyes. 'I didn't expect it 'ud be so 'ot,' he gasped. 'It never is in these places.'

Gordan took out a packet of Players and helped himself to a cigarette. 'No good offering you one of these?' he said, holding out the packet.

'No, thanks, Mr. Cross. I'll 'ave one o' me own cigars.'

'Not here you won't!' exclaimed Gordan in alarm. 'I've smelt those cigars of yours before, and the fumes are lethal. We shall be thrown out!'

Mr. Budd sighed. 'I can't understand why people don't like 'em,' he said plaintively.

'They're very special — there's only one place in London where yer can get 'em.'

'I can well believe it. A rope factory, I should imagine. Look here, do you think Marsh is Midnight?'

The big man rubbed his chin thoughtfully. 'Maybe,' he said noncommittally.

'If Marsh was broke three years ago, where did he get his money to buy all this property?'

'You think he got it from the proceeds of all these robberies?'

'Yes, I do.'

'Probably you're right, but 'ow are yer goin' to prove it?'

'Find out where the money *did* come from. If it was from some legitimate source, it shouldn't be difficult to discover where. Who's Marsh's lawyer?'

'Now I can tell yer that,' said Mr. Budd, as though it was a very surprising thing that he should be able to tell anybody anything. 'A feller named Snood. The firm's called Snood, Fender, Hickson and Snood. You won't get any information out of old Snood. He's a wily old devil and close as an oyster.'

'You sound as though you'd had dealings with him before.'

'I have,' answered Mr. Budd grimly.

'Is he straight?'

'Nothin's ever been proved against him.'

'Which means that he isn't.' Gordan nodded. 'You don't think it would be any use trying to get out of him where Marsh's money came from?'

'Not without a warrant,' said the big man, shaking his head. 'an' we wouldn't get that — not unless we could prove that Marsh was guilty of somethin' criminal.'

Gordan finished his coffee and pushed aside the cup. 'Williams knows something about Marsh. I wonder if he could be persuaded to talk.'

Mr. Budd looked dubious. 'He's a queer feller,' he replied after a pause. 'You won't get anythin' out of him that 'e don't want to tell.'

'I might,' said Gordan, remembering a certain Lew Steiner.

Mr. Budd's sleepy eyes became suddenly shrewd. 'Well,' he remarked, 'I don't 'old with puttin' the black on a feller, but p'raps in a good cause . . . '

'Who said anything about blackmail?'

'Nobody,' answered the big man innocently. 'I was just makin' a remark, that's all.' He looked at his watch. 'I must be gettin' back to the Yard,' he said, struggling to his feet and reaching for his hat. 'If you think you can get anythin' out o' Williams, try it. I'll be interested to 'ear what happens.' He felt in his waistcoat pocket, produced one of his black cigars, and stuck it between his teeth. 'Real tobacco,' he said appreciatively. 'I won't light it till I get outside.' He nodded and lumbered heavily over to the door.

Gordan watched him pause outside the tea shop and light his cigar. He was moving away when there was the sudden tinkle of breaking glass — then the big man clapped a hand to the side of his head, stumbled, and fell heavily to the pavement.

Gordan was momentarily stunned by the suddenness of the thing, and then he sprang to his feet and ran to the door. Several people who were passing stopped to see what the matter was as he bent over the prone figure of the big man. There was a trickle of red running down the side of Mr. Budd's face from a furrow across the left temple — a nasty gash, but not serious.

'What happened?' asked Gordan as he helped the superintendent to his feet.

'Somebody shot at me,' answered Mr. Budd shakily. He was dazed and a little dizzy.

'Somebody from a car that was waitin' on the other side of the street.'

'I know; the bullet smashed the window. How do you feel?'

'Not too bad,' murmured Mr. Budd, gingerly touching the side of his head. 'Bit of an 'eadache an' not too steady on me legs, but I'll be all right in a minute.'

'Did you see who it was?'

The big man started to shake his head and winced. 'No; it all 'appened too quickly.'

By now a fair-sized crowd had gathered, and a policeman forced his way through its gaping ranks. 'Now then,' he demanded, 'what's goin' on here?'

'All right, Constable,' said Mr. Budd. He produced his warrant card, and the suspicion faded from the policeman's eyes.

'Are you badly hurt, sir?' he asked anxiously.

'No, only a scratch. Get all these people away.'

The crowd dispersed before authority, and Mr. Budd explained what had happened. 'Which direction did you come from, Constable?' he asked.

The constable pointed up the street.

'Did you see a dark green Morgan-Riley saloon pass you?'

'Yes, sir. Going pretty fast, it was.'

'Did you see who was driving it?'

The constable shook his head. He had had no particular reason for taking notice of the driver. It was a man; that was all he could say. His face showed his bitter disappointment. Here was a chance for promotion, and he had missed it.

'I didn't hear any sound of a shot,' said Gordan.

'They used a silencer or a powerful air-pistol,' said Mr. Budd.

The manageress of the tea shop was demanding to know what was going to be done about the window, and the superintendent turned her over to the constable to deal with. 'Come on, Mr. Cross,' he said. 'Let's get out of this.'

The taxi took them to Scotland Yard, where Mr. Budd had the wound in his temple attended to. When later he sat facing Gordan across the desk in his cheerless office, he looked little the worse for his adventure.

'There's no doubt the shooter was someone ter do with this business,' he remarked. 'Prob'bly the same feller who shot at you at that bungalow.'

'And instigated by Sir Franklin Marsh,' said Gordan.

'Seems more'n likely.'

'We must have been followed when we left Sir Franklin's house, and they waited for us coming out of the tea shop.'

'Silly thin' ter do,' murmured the big man, gazing sleepily at the ceiling. 'What did they 'ope to gain?'

'They hoped to put you out of the case. That's obvious.'

'I know, but why? Another man would've been put on. What good would it 'ave done 'em?'

'Perhaps they think you know more than you do. If Mr. Midnight *is* Marsh, our visit there this morning probably produced a strong vertical breeze. He got scared and sent one of his thugs to make sure we wouldn't be any further trouble. They expected us to leave that tea shop together.'

'Well,' remarked Mr. Budd, shifting to a more comfortable position in his chair, 'we're up against a deadlock.' He took a cigar from his waistcoat pocket, sniffed at it, caught the expression on Gordan's face, and reluctantly put it back again with a sigh. 'There isn't very much to go on,' he continued slowly, fixing his eyes on the ceiling. 'If we could find out 'ow that woman, Myra Destry, comes into it, we might get somewhere.'

'Or what she meant by that reference to an Intaglio ring.'

'Ah,' said Mr. Budd, 'maybe that woman, Audrey Smith, could tell us somethin' about that. There's another mystery — who's she an' what is she mixed up in this business for?' He shook his head. 'Nothin' but queer people an' happenings in this case — nothin' straightforward. Look at these Destrys at Evesham Mansions. Who are they? There's a connection between them and the dead woman — she gave you their address, an' we find that she was livin' in a bungalow that was rented by Destry.'

'But which really belongs to Sir

Franklin Marsh.'

'Don't keep on interruptin',' grunted the big man irritably. 'It breaks my train o' thought. As I was sayin', there's a connection between these Destry people an' the dead woman. The question is, what was it? an' then we've got this feller Patrella, an' that singin' chap Mayne, an' the band leader Castell.'

'You haven't got him,' murmured Gordan. 'He's dead.'

'That was a figure o' speech,' said Mr. Budd loftily. 'You know very well what I mean. I'm talkin' about all these people bein' mixed up in this business. You can't sort out what they've got to do with it.'

'Find Mr. Midnight, and all the rest will be clear.'

'That's easier said than done. Accordin' to that notebook o' the dead woman's, 'e's one o' these people I've mentioned — but which one?' Mr. Budd rubbed his chin and sighed. 'Whichever way you look at it, it's a mix-up, an' I don't see what to do about it.'

'I suggest that you put somebody on to keep an eye on Marsh. I'm pretty sure that if he isn't Mr. Midnight, he knows all about him.'

Mr. Budd considered this. 'I'll get Leek on the job,' he said after a long pause. 'In the meanwhile, it 'ud be a good idea if you could get 'old of Williams an' see what you can get out of him. Most of the information we've got up to now 'as come from 'im.'

'I'll try,' said Gordan. He got up and stretched himself. 'Are you going to be here all day if I want to get in touch with you?'

Mr. Budd put his feet up on the desk and settled back in his chair. 'I'll be 'ere. I'm goin' to put in a good hour or so thinkin'.'

He closed his eyes, and the last Gordan saw of him as he left the office, he was in the act of putting one of the evil-looking black cigars he was so fond of between his lips.

12

After leaving Scotland Yard, Gordan Cross made his way to the offices of the *Clarion*. He settled himself down at a typewriter in the reporters' room and hammered out a couple of columns about the murder and the sensational discovery of Castell's body in the boat at the bungalow. He made no mention of the fact that the dead woman had been living there, nor did he make any reference to Destry's visit or the presence of the unknown man who had shot at them.

It was a very tame and noncommittal article, and Tully was not slow to comment on the fact when he glanced through Gordan's copy. 'Can't you do anything better than this?' he grunted, looking up.

'Not yet,' answered Gordan. 'You'll have all the sensation you want, J.T., presently.'

'I hope so. This is all very well as a fill-in, but what I want is more about this fellow Mr. Midnight. *He*'s the story, and you haven't even mentioned him.'

'Be patient. You'll have so much about him soon that you'll have to print a special edition to get it all in.'

Gordan went back to his flat, to find that Vicky was out. He concluded that she had probably gone shopping. He made himself some coffee, settled himself comfortably in the sitting-room, and put in a little intense thinking. When Vicky came in a couple of hours later, he was fast asleep.

'How the gentlemen of the press overwork themselves to find news for the great unappreciative public,' said Vicky sarcastically. 'If you go on like this, you'll have a breakdown!'

He blinked up at her. 'There are times when a policy of masterly inactivity is best.'

'That would impress me more if it didn't happen so often. What you really mean is that you're stumped.'

'Not at all,' he retorted, getting up and yawning. 'It'd be a very good thing if you had a little rest yourself. You've got a late night before you.'

'Why?' she asked eagerly. 'What are we going to do?'

'We're going to that haunt of expensive vice, The Yellow Orchid,' he answered, lighting a cigarette. 'We shall eat, drink and be merry far into the small hours.'

Her eyes sparkled. 'That suits me. There's nothing I should like better. What time are we going?'

'I think you'd better meet me there at half-past nine.'

'Why can't we go together?'

'I shan't have time to come here and pick you up.'

'Where are you going?'

'I want to try and find Nosey Williams. You go to The Yellow Orchid — I'll book a table — and wait there until I join you.'

'I don't like going there on my own,' she said, frowning. 'Why can't I meet you somewhere?'

'Because I can't make sure of being anywhere at a fixed time. It all depends how long it'll take me to find Williams, and how long I'll be with him when I do. You'll be all right at The Yellow Orchid.'

'I hope so. How am I going to get there?'

'You'd better hire a car.'

She made a grimace. 'That's going to cost something — or will it figure on your expense sheet?'

'It'll figure on my expense sheet.' Gordan refrained from adding that he hoped the eagle-eyed John Tully would pass it.

He telephoned to The Yellow Orchid, spoke to the head waiter, and succeeded in reserving a table for two. He wondered, as he replaced the telephone on its rack, whether the excitable Mr. Patrella and his taciturn friend Mr. Macbane would be there. He rather thought they would. That was one of the reasons why he was going. The other reason was more in the nature of a gamble, but there was a chance it might come off. He kept this second reason to himself, however, concluding that Vicky might not altogether approve.

It was dusk when he took out his little car from the garage at the corner of the road and set off in search of Nosey Williams. But he failed to find that wizened little man. He called at all Williams's usual haunts, but the informer

164

was not at any of them, nor had he been seen. Gordan came last to The Pewter Pot. This was not one of Nosey's recognized haunts, but the reporter thought as he had used it before, he might be there. Once more, however, he drew a blank. There were very few people in the bar, and Nosey was not one of them. He seemed to be making himself scarce. Gordan remembered the terror in his voice when he had rung up and made his last appointment, and wondered if he had gone into hiding from somebody. That he had been afraid at that last meeting had been obvious.

There was nothing he could do but give it up. He had no idea where the informer lived. He had always been very reticent about that. It was doubtful if even the police knew. Gordan thought that a man who carried on such an unsavoury profession was perhaps wise to keep his address a secret. There were many who would like to get one back on Nosey Williams.

It had begun to rain again as he sped along towards The Yellow Orchid, his screen-wiper working madly. He wondered how Vicky was getting on. She must have been there for nearly an hour if she had got there at half-past nine. It was nearly ten-thirty. She wouldn't be pleased at having to wait.

It was a quarter to eleven when he drew up outside the roadhouse, parked his car, and hurried inside. He left his coat and hat in the cloakroom and passed on into the main part of the club. The lights were low and Rodney Mayne was singing, bathed in a pinkish-hued spotlight. The song was very sentimental and sugary. Mayne's voice quavered and throbbed in the extremity of his despair over the loss of somebody named, with startling originality, Honey. The band, under a new leader, wailed an accompaniment that seemed to have nothing at all to do with the melody that Mayne was crooning.

Gordan tried to find Vicky, but the gloom was too great, and he could not see where she was sitting. He leant back against the wall near the entrance until such time as Rodney Mayne should have ceased his lachrymose lament, unwilling to disturb the hushed rhapsody with which it was being received.

It ended at last amid a burst of applause, the lights went up, Mayne bowed, withdrew, and the band plunged into a quick step. Gordan saw Vicky. She was sitting at a table on the other side of the dance floor, and he made his way through the dancers towards her.

'Here I am at last,' he greeted her as he sat down at the table.

'About time, too. I thought you were never coming. What happened? Did you find Williams?'

'No; I drew a complete blank. He hasn't been seen since I met him that night in The Pewter Pot.'

'Well, the least you can do after keeping me hanging about here all on my own is to buy me some supper. I've had three gin and limes, and it's made me hungry.'

Gordan sighed. 'You're an expensive person to take out. Old Tully'll never stand for your supper on the expense sheet.'

'Then you can pay for it out of your own pocket,' declared Vicky. 'The food looks very good. Those people over there have had duckling, and it looked delicious.'

Gordan was hungry himself. He looked round and beckoned to a waiter. The man came quickly — the service at The Yellow Orchid was remarkably good — and took his order. The wine waiter, seeing a possible customer, hurried up and presented his list with deference, and was a little disappointed when Gordan ordered iced lager and a Booth's gin and lime.

While he waited for the meal to be brought, Gordan looked round the crowded room. The Yellow Orchid was fairly full. Nearly all the tables round the small dance floor were occupied, or showed signs of occupation in cloaks and handbags that had been left while their owners danced. Patrella was sitting at a table a short distance away, talking very earnestly to Macbane; and standing by the bar was Sir Franklin Marsh, talking to a tall dark woman who was wearing a great deal of jewellery.

Patrella looked up suddenly — Gordan was under the impression that Macbane had said something, but he couldn't be sure — smiled a greeting, and waved his hand. He acknowledged the salutation with a nod, and Patrella turned back to his companion and continued his animated conversation.

A waiter appeared with their drinks on a tray — not the waiter who had taken the order, but a different man. Gordan might have taken very little notice of him if he hadn't seen something that attracted his attention as the man set down the drinks on the table.

On the third finger of his right hand, he wore a very fine Intaglio ring!

Gordan saw that Vicky had seen it, too. He looked up, eyeing the man with suddenly awakened interest. He was slim and dark, and good-looking in a foreign, rather Spanish way. His hair was very smooth and brushed back over a well-shaped head. Above his upper lip was a thin line of moustache. He smiled, his lips parting to show a dazzling array of teeth, but the smile never touched his eyes, which remained cold and expressionless.

'That's a very fine ring you're wearing,' remarked Gordan.

'You like it?' replied the man. He held out the hand with the ring, displaying it with evident pride. 'It ees ver' beautiful, I think. It belong to my mother. I would not part with it for much money.'

'You're very sensible,' said Gordan. 'That type of ring isn't very common.'

'Not common at all,' agreed the waiter. 'Not so fine as theese. I have seen others, but . . . ' He shrugged his shoulders expressively.

'I've seen somebody else here with a ring like that,' remarked Vicky. 'I can't remember who it was.'

'I think you mistake, madam,' said the waiter. 'I do not know of any other with a ring like theese.'

'I'm quite sure I've seen someone,' said Vicky, 'and I'm quite sure it was here. I remember — it was a man who was with that woman who was killed, what was her name? Destry — Myra Destry.'

The smile vanished from the waiter's face. His eyes grew suddenly suspicious and wary. 'You mistake,' he repeated, bowed and hurried away.

'You shouldn't have said that, Vicky,' said Gordan. 'You've scared him!'

'I wanted to see what his reaction

would be,' she answered.

'Well, you have. What do you make of it?'

'Myra Destry mentioned an Intaglio ring just before she died, and she mentioned it again in that notebook. There's something important about that ring, Gordan!'

'She might not have been referring to this one. I suppose there are others.'

'It's rather a peculiar coincidence, though, you must admit that,' she said. 'Myra Destry attaches so much importance to an Intaglio ring that she mentions it with her dying breath, and we find one worn by a waiter in this place — *this* place, Gordan!'

'Oh, I know,' he interrupted quickly. 'But a waiter?'

'He may be a waiter some of the time,' said Vicky, 'but what is he when he isn't waiting?'

'I suppose you're suggesting he's Mr. Midnight?'

'Well, why not? You don't know who Mr. Midnight is, or anything about him. For all you know, he might hide himself under the guise of a waiter. Don't forget,' she went on quickly as he opened his mouth to speak, 'that card that we found under the ashtray. Who could have put it there more easily than a waiter?'

'There's a lot in what you say,' murmured Gordan, 'but I can't believe that.'

A sharp kick on the shin from Vicky made him stop and look up. Rodney Mayne had approached their table. He looked pale and worried.

'Good evening,' he said. 'I thought it was you, Mrs. Cross, but I wasn't certain until your husband joined you, otherwise I should have come over before. May I sit down for a moment?'

'Do,' said Vicky.

Mayne dragged forward a chair from a nearby table and sat down between them. 'Marsh told me about poor Castell,' he said abruptly. 'It's terrible, isn't it? Have you any idea who killed him, Mr. Cross?'

'Only that it was undoubtedly the same person who killed Myra Destry,' answered Gordan. He took a packet of Players from his pocket and offered Mayne a cigarette. The crooner took one and tapped it gently on his thumbnail.

'What do the police think?' he asked. 'Have they any idea who it was?'

Gordan shook his head. He held out his lighter and Mayne took it, snapping the little flame to life nervously. He appeared to be very worried and upset, which, Gordan supposed, was only natural. After all, Castell had been an intimate friend.

'There's hardly been time for the police to come to any conclusion, has there?' said Vicky.

'No, I suppose not.' Mayne twisted the cigarette about in his long fingers. 'I was wondering if you'd heard anything.'

'Nothing definite at present,' said Gordan.

Mayne took a long pull at his cigarette, inhaled the smoke deeply, and slowly expelled it. They got an impression that he wanted to say something and was trying to make up his mind how to begin. 'Drewitt has taken over the band temporarily,' he said after a pause. 'I don't know what will happen eventually — perhaps they'll get another band.'

'Were you under contract to Castell?' asked Gordan.

'Yes, we all were. Marsh paid a lump

sum to Laddie, and he paid us. I don't know what will happen if he gets a new band. We'll all go, I suppose.'

Gordan glanced over at the rostrum. The band was playing a foxtrot, and seemed to be as efficient as they had been under Laddie Castell's leadership. Drewitt appeared to be quite capable of carrying on. He said as much, and Mayne agreed.

'That's what we're hoping will happen,' he said. 'If Marsh will transfer the contract to Drewitt, we'll just carry on as before. I think that'd be the best thing to do, but it rests entirely with Marsh.'

'What's the name of the assistant wine waiter?' asked Gordan.

Mayne looked surprised. 'The assistant wine waiter?'

'Yes, he's over there,' said Vicky, 'serving those people.'

Rodney Mayne followed the direction of her eyes. 'I don't know. I've never seen him before. He must be new.'

'He's wearing a rather lovely ring,' said Vicky. 'An Intaglio.'

'What's the matter, Mr. Mayne?' broke in Gordan quickly, for the singer had started and dropped his cigarette on to the tablecloth.

'Nothing,' answered Mayne. He picked up the burning cigarette and stubbed it out in the ashtray. 'Your wife mentioning the ring like that startled me.'

'Why?' asked Vicky.

'Because Castell was asking about an Intaglio ring on the night he went to keep that appointment with Myra at Elsinore Lodge,' replied Mayne. 'He asked me if I'd ever seen anyone in the club wearing one.'

'And had you?' asked Gordan.

'I told him I had. He got quite excited.'

'Who did you see wearing an Intaglio ring here?' asked Gordan.

'Sir Franklin Marsh,' said Rodney Mayne.

13

Vicky drew in her breath sharply and looked quickly at Gordan. 'Sir Franklin Marsh,' she repeated softly.

'That's very interesting,' remarked Gordan, trying to keep the excitement out of his voice. 'I've never noticed that he wore an Intaglio ring.'

'He doesn't now,' said Mayne. 'But he used to.'

'When did he give up wearing it?' asked the reporter.

'Oh, it's a long time now. I'd almost forgotten he ever did, when Castell asked me. It was when he first opened this place.'

'And he suddenly stopped wearing the ring?' murmured Gordan.

'Well, I've never seen him with it since,' said Mayne. He looked curiously from one to the other. 'Why are you so interested?'

'Gordan's always promised to buy me an Intaglio ring,' said Vicky quite untruthfully. 'I've always been terribly fond of them. They're not very easy to find, you know.'

'I've seen plenty of them,' said Mayne. 'They've got a lot in that shop in New Oxford Street, and I've seen several in one or two other places.'

'Not very good specimens,' put in Gordan hastily. 'The really good ones are quite rare.'

'Oh, well, I expect you know more about that than I do,' said Mayne. He got up. 'I must go — I've got another number to do in a few minutes.' He nodded to Gordan, bowed to Vicky, and made his way over to the band dais. A waiter arrived with their supper at that moment, and they were forced to talk about nothing in particular until the man had gone.

'What do you think of that?' asked Vicky when they were once more alone. 'Sir Franklin Marsh, eh?'

'I think it's a far better bet than an unknown little wine waiter,' said Gordan, helping her to green peas. 'Sauteed potatoes?'

'You can give me some more of those peas first,' she said. 'I'm not letting you get away with two-thirds of them.'

'You know,' Gordan went on, 'it's a very queer coincidence about that ring. Have you ever seen a waiter with such a ring before?'

Vicky frowned, wrinkling her nose. It was an attractive little habit she had when she was puzzled. 'No, I don't think I have,' she said. 'What do you mean?'

'I was wondering whether that ring wasn't shown to us on purpose.'

'How could it have been?'

'Well, they knew we were coming here tonight. I booked a table. Maybe Marsh arranged for that waiter to wear the ring for our special benefit.'

'He said it belonged to his mother.'

'I know. He may have been instructed to say that. You heard what Mayne said? He's a new man. Supposing Marsh wanted to be somebody to seen wearing an Intaglio ring?'

'So that we wouldn't look any further? Is that what you mean?'

Gordan nodded, his mouth full of roast duckling.

'A kind of stooge,' went on Vicky. 'I

think there might be something in that, Gordan.'

'Marsh used to wear an Intaglio ring, but he suddenly gave up wearing it. Myra Destry associated an Intaglio ring in some way with Mr. Midnight.'

'How did *Marsh* know that?' she said. 'She mentioned an Intaglio ring to you just before she died, and she wrote something about a ring in that notebook, but how did Marsh know?'

'I can't tell you, but I'm just supposing that he did. He's afraid that the ring might supply a clue, so he gives up wearing it; and in case anybody should be looking for a man wearing that type of ring, he sees to it that there *is* such a man, hoping that it will block any further inquiries.'

'Wouldn't that put him in the hands of the man?'

'Oh, I've no doubt that he offered quite a plausible reason,' said Gordan. 'Perhaps he's got some kind of a hold over the man, and blackmailed him into doing what he wanted.'

'It would still put Marsh rather in his power, wouldn't it?'

'Yes, and that's where we may be able to get hold of some useful information. If we can scare the man into telling us what he knows, it might provide us with some proof against Marsh. That's all Budd wants to work on — something that definitely involves Marsh in this business.'

He let his eyes rove round the crowded room, but there was no sign of the wine waiter. His chief was busily engaged in opening a bottle of champagne for a party at a table near the band dais, but of the other waiter there was no sign.

Patrella and the dour Macbane were still sitting at their table, but they were no longer talking animatedly. They seemed to be rather disinterestedly watching the dancers. Sir Franklin Marsh and the woman he had been talking to at the bar had disappeared.

With a preliminary roll on the drums, the new band leader introduced Rodney Mayne. The lights dimmed, the spotlight focused on the crooner as he stepped to the front of the platform behind the microphone, and he began to sing. It was the same type of song as he had sung before, a heartbreaking lyric all about a woman who was now 'only a dream in the night'. It went down very well, and Mayne had to do an encore. When this was over and the lights went up again, Gordan had another look round for the waiter with the ring, but he was still absent. Nor did he show up again. It was as though he had been engaged to perform a particular part, and having performed it, had taken his departure.

Gordan and Vicky lingered until the small hours in the hope that he might return, but at last they were so tired that they had to go; and anyway, the band were playing the last waltz.

On the way home, Vicky fell asleep, leaning her head against Gordan's shoulder. He pulled her cloak round her, for the night was cold and damp. He had wanted her to get in the back when they started, but she had preferred to sit beside him, protesting that it was warmer.

It had not been an altogether unproductive evening, he thought as he drove through the deserted streets. He had failed to find Nosey Williams, and he had not been able to do all that he had intended at The Yellow Orchid, but there was the compensation of the ring.

He had a feeling that this was more important than anything else, and he was determined to find the waiter and get the truth concerning the ring out of him.

It was striking three when he brought the car to a stop outside the block of flats where they lived. 'Wake up, darling,' he said gently. 'We're home.'

Vicky stirred and opened her eyes. 'Oh,' she murmured huskily, 'I'm so tired.'

'Well, it won't be long before you're in bed. Hop out. I'll just put the car away.'

She got out, yawning. Halfway across the pavement, she remembered that she had left her evening bag behind. It had dropped off her lap. 'It must be somewhere just down beside you,' she said.

Gordan felt about on the floor near his feet and found the bag. 'Here you are,' he said. 'Now hurry up and get into bed. I won't be long.' He stopped as he heard the sudden hissing intake of her breath.

'Look,' she whispered. 'Gordan, look!'

She was staring at the little white suede bag in her hand — only it was no longer white. 'It's blood,' she said, and there was a shrill edge of horror in her voice. 'It's blood!'

'Nonsense!' exclaimed Gordan. 'How could it be? You've just got lipstick over it.'

'Look at your *hand*,' she broke in. 'Is *that* lipstick?'

Gordan switched on the dashboard light and looked at his fingers. They were red and sticky. 'It *is* blood,' he said. 'Where the devil did it come from?'

'It's all over my bag. It must be on the floor.'

He bent down. It was dark and difficult to see, and he pulled out his lighter. In the light from the little flame, he made out a dark patch on the shabby carpet. It glistened, and when he touched it, it was wet. Gordan opened the other door and scrambled out of the car.

'It appears to have seeped through from the back,' he said, coming round and joining Vicky on the pavement. 'You'd better go on up to the flat.'

'I'm not going until I know where that blood came from,' she declared. 'Where *could* it have come from?'

'I don't know. But I'm afraid there's something rather horrible in the back. I wish you'd go!'

'I'm not going until I know.'

He knew that when she adopted that tone it was useless to argue further. With a queer, uneasy feeling in the pit of his stomach, he opened the rear door of the car and peered inside. Something that looked like a heap of rugs filled the space between the back seat and the bucket-seats in front. He saw a dim glimmer of white. Once again he snapped his lighter into flame, and then he saw more clearly.

'What is it?' whispered Vicky, close behind him.

He turned round, and she saw that his face had gone very pale.

'It's the waiter,' he replied huskily. 'We shan't get any information out of him. He's dead!'

★ ★ ★

'They must have killed him and put his body in the back of the car while we were having supper,' said Gordan. 'They wanted to make sure he couldn't be questioned about that ring.'

Mr. Budd rubbed his chin wearily. He looked very tired. Once again, he had been dragged from his bed in the small hours of the morning by an urgent telephone call from Gordan Cross, and gone through all the preliminary routine inquiries that immediately followed the discovery of a murder: the cause of death, identity of the body, police photographs, all the wearisome and numberless little items that had to be attended to at the beginning of a murder inquiry. The cause of death had been a knife wound in the back which had penetrated the heart, and the identity of the dead man had been established from the contents of his pockets.

His name was Beppo Ricardi, and he was an Italian. His address was a boarding-house in Soho. The landlady, also an Italian, had been forced to view the body of her erstwhile lodger at the mortuary to which it had been taken. She had declared without hesitation that it was Beppo Ricardi, which tallied with the name on the dead man's ration book. Still volubly protesting, partly in Italian and partly in her own particular brand of English, the woman had been allowed to return to her house, but accompanied by the melancholy Leek — also hurriedly roused from his slumbers — who had strict instructions to make a thorough search of the room occupied by Ricardi, seal it up, and leave a police constable on guard.

When all this and a great deal more had been attended to, Mr. Budd had returned to Gordan's flat and, fortified by coffee, had listened while the reporter gave a detailed account of his meeting with Ricardi at The Yellow Orchid.

'There was no ring on his finger when we examined the body,' said the superintendent. 'You know that?'

'Yes; that was the first thing I noticed. They must have taken it off after they killed him.'

'Who's 'they'?' demanded Mr. Budd, irritably pulling at his nose. 'That's the question.'

'Sir Franklin Marsh for one,' said Vicky.

Mr. Budd made an impatient gesture. 'You think so. *I* think so. But what proof have we got? I'll tell yer — none!'

'Mayne says Marsh used to wear an Intaglio ring,' said Gordan.

'So what?' grunted the big man. 'Supposin' 'e did — there are 'undreds of men wearin' Intaglio rings.'

'You must admit it's a very peculiar coincidence about the ring,' put in Vicky. 'There must be a very good reason why Marsh gave up wearing the ring suddenly, why this waiter was wearing one and had it taken from his body, and why Myra Destry mentioned a ring just before she died and made a note about one in that book.'

'Of course there's a reason,' said Mr. Budd. 'An' it's probably the reason you and I think it is, but it doesn't 'elp me. I can't go an' question Marsh about the ring.'

'Why not?' she demanded.

'Because 'e'd put in a complaint to the commissioner as like as not, an' 'e'd be within 'is rights. I could ask him if 'e'd ever worn a ring of that type, an' why 'e suddenly stopped wearin' it, and 'e could tell me to mind my own business. What good would that do?'

'I'm quite sure that Sir Franklin Marsh is at the bottom of the whole thing, all the same,' said Gordan.

'An' I agree with you,' said Mr. Budd. 'Just give me one little, tiny bit o' solid proof that 'e is, an' I'll go for 'im bald-'eaded. But without it my hands are tied.' He passed a huge hand across his face with a weary gesture.

'There's one way we could catch him,' said Gordan. 'If we could find out when next he's going to arrange one of his midnight pay-outs, and where we could catch him red-handed.'

'The only person who'd be able to tell us that,' grunted Mr. Budd, 'is Nosey Williams.'

'And he's vanished,' interrupted Gordan. 'I searched everywhere for him last night without result.'

'Maybe 'e'll turn up again,' said the big man. ''E's our best bet, Mr. Cross. 'E knows all about Mr. Midnight — we'd never 'ave known the feller existed but for Williams.'

'He swore he didn't know who he is,' said Gordan.

'Maybe 'e was speakin' the truth, maybe 'e wasn't. But 'e could find out — Nosey could find out anythin'. It's not only 'is business, but it's an 'obby. 'E just can't 'elp pokin' that queer nose of 'is inter thin's, an' very useful it's been to us in the past.'

'I think he's keeping out of the way because he's scared,' said Gordan. 'He gave me the impression of being frightened to death when I saw him last.'

'P'raps 'e 'as good cause ter be scared. You 'aven't seen anythin' more of this woman Smith, 'ave you?'

'No,' answered Gordan. 'She's vanished, too.'

'P'raps they've gone off together,' said Mr. Budd with heavy humour. 'I must do a bit o' vanishin' meself,' he added, extricating himself from his chair with much difficulty. 'I've got a lot ter do, an' it won't get done sittin 'ere talkin' an' drinkin' coffee.'

The ringing of the telephone bell interrupted him. Vicky, who was nearest the instrument, picked up the receiver.

'Hello?' she said. 'Yes, this is Mr. Cross's flat.' She turned to Gordan. 'Someone wants you,' she said. He went over and took the receiver from her hand.

'Cross speaking. Who is it?'

'Just a minute,' answered a man's voice. There was a short pause, and then a woman's voice came on the line.

'Good morning, Mr. Cross,' it said. 'This is Audrey Smith, do you remember?'

14

Gordan covered the mouthpiece of the telephone with his hand. 'Audrey Smith is on the line now,' he said hurriedly; and then, removing his hand: 'Of course I remember. I was wondering when you were going to turn up again.'

'I'm sure you were,' she answered. 'Listen, can you meet me at Russell Square Tube station in half an hour?'

Gordan glanced at his watch. It was barely a quarter to seven. 'You keep early hours.'

'You're not going to tell me that you're in bed, Mr. Cross?' she said mockingly. 'After the excitement of last night, I couldn't believe that.'

'What do you know about the excitement of last night?' he asked quickly.

'You'd be surprised. Can you meet me?'

'Why don't you come here?'

'There are several reasons. Russell

Square Tube station in half an hour.' Before he had time to reply, she had rung off.

'I'd rather like to meet this Audrey Smith,' said Mr. Budd when Gordan told him the gist of the conversation.

'Why not come along with me?' said Gordan.

The big man considered this thoughtfully. 'Maybe it 'ud scare 'er off,' he said dubiously. 'I tell yer what — you go an' meet 'er on your own, an' I'll drop into that tea shop just round the corner in Southampton Row. If you could persuade 'er to come in there, well then we could meet accidentally like, see?'

Gordan saw and agreed. Mr. Budd took his departure, and at twenty minutes past seven, Gordan set off for Russell Square Tube station. It was a cold, damp morning with a promise of more rain in the leaden sky. The early workers were hurrying into the station, morose and sleepy-eyed for the most part, though there were one or two who appeared more cheerful and indulged in some good-humoured chaff as they crowded into the lift.

192

Gordan took up his position by the bookstall and waited. It was exactly half-past seven when a cab stopped in front of the station and the slim figure of Audrey Smith got out. She paid the driver, gave a quick glance round, and came over to Gordan.

'Good morning,' she said brightly.

'Good morning,' he answered. 'This is rather an early hour for an appointment, isn't it?'

'What's time?' she said.

'It can be all sorts of things,' he replied. 'Pleasant, unpleasant, or just a nuisance.'

'And also something you can't mess about with,' she said. All the while she was speaking, her eyes kept darting left and right, over his shoulder and behind her.

'Are you looking for someone?' he asked.

She shook her head. 'I'm making sure that someone isn't there.'

'Who?'

'Never mind. Let's go someplace where we can talk.'

'There's a tea shop quite near,' said

193

Gordan. 'It usually opens very early for breakfasts. We could get a cup of coffee.'

'That'll do. Let's go.'

He led the way into Southampton Row and turned to the left. The tea shop that Mr. Budd had mentioned was a few yards down on the left-hand side.

'Is he waiting there, or is he coming in a few minutes after us?' asked Miss Smith calmly as they reached the door.

'What do you mean?' asked Gordan, taken completely by surprise.

'Superintendent Budd,' she answered. She saw the consternation on his face, and laughed.

'How on earth did you know?'

'I didn't,' she retorted coolly, 'but I do now. I thought it was possible he might have been still with you when I telephoned, and that you might have arranged something like this. You must have told him about me, and he'd naturally be curious. It was a shot in the dark, but it hit the target, didn't it?'

'He's waiting inside,' said Gordan. This woman who looked so dainty and feminine was no fool, he thought as he pushed open the door of the tea shop. You'd have to get up very, very early to get the better of her.

The place was almost empty. One or two people sat at the small tables having breakfast, but the majority would come in later. From eight until half-past nine would be the peak time.

Mr. Budd was sitting at a table at the far end, sleepily contemplating a cup of coffee. He looked up as they came over.

'Good morning, Superintendent,' greeted Audrey Smith. 'I thought we should find you here.' She sat down.

'Oh, you did, eh?' remarked Mr. Budd in his deep rumble.

'I didn't tell her,' said Gordan. 'She told me!'

'I s'pose,' said the big man, eyeing her with interest, 'that you're 'A. Smith'?'

'That's right,' she answered with a smile. 'The 'A' stands for Audrey.'

'An' what do *you* stand for?' inquired Mr. Budd, tugging gently at one ear. ''Ow do you come into this business of robbery an' murder an' receivin' of stolen property? You look a nice sort o' gal.'

'I'm an exceedingly nice sort,' she declared gravely. 'Can we have some coffee?'

'I'll get it,' said Gordan. 'Do you want another cup?' Mr. Budd, to whom the question had been addressed, shook his large head.

'No more for me,' he said. 'One cup o' this stuffs enough. Coffee!' He made an expressive grimace.

Gordan laughed and went over to the long counter that ran across the end of the tea shop, which was one of those 'help yourself' arrangements. He came back with two cups of coffee, set them down on the table, and pulled up a chair. 'Now,' he said, 'why did you want to see me so early?'

Audrey Smith stirred her coffee slowly. She appeared to be thinking out the best way to begin. Mr. Budd, his sleepy eyes watching her, wondered how she came into the business at all.

'Before I say anything,' she began at last, 'you must promise not to ask questions.'

'That's goin' to be a bit difficult, miss,' grunted the big man. 'It's my business to ask questions.'

'It's not my business to answer them,' she retorted. 'I'm doing my best to help, but I must be allowed to do it in my own way.'

'That's all very well, miss, but if you know anything that's likely to 'elp the police, it's your duty to.'

'I'm perfectly aware of my duty,' broke in Audrey Smith calmly. 'I'm doing it.'

Mr. Budd sighed. 'You know what I ought to do?' he said. 'I ought to — '

'Arrest me?' she said, her eyes twinkling. 'You can if you like. But if you do, you'll only have to release me again, and you won't hear what I've got to say. It's entirely up to you — you can please yourself.'

The big man looked at her, smiling pleasantly across the little table at him, and he came to the same conclusion that Gordan had earlier. This woman had all her wits about her. She wasn't afraid of anything he could do, and she was right because there was very little he *could* do. He could arrest her, it was true, but he had very little against her. She seemed to know quite a lot about these people who were all mixed up with the Midnight business, but he couldn't prove that she had anything to do with it, and it was more probable that, as she said, he would only have to release her again. Maybe there was more to be gained by letting her run it her own way.

'All right,' he said wearily. 'I'll just listen.'

'Then here's what I've got to say.' She leaned closer and dropped her voice. 'You want to find this man who calls himself Mr. Midnight, don't you?'

'Do you know who 'e is?' asked Mr. Budd.

'I know where you can find him at twelve o'clock tonight.'

'Where?' asked Gordan.

'If you'll meet me at ten o'clock at Battersea Park station,' she said, 'I'll take you to the place. You'd better bring some men with you, and see that they're armed. When you get him in a corner, he's likely to be dangerous.'

They tried very hard to extract more information from her, but she refused. 'I can't tell you any more now,' she said

198

obstinately. 'I told you I wasn't answering any questions.'

'Surely you can tell us where this place is?' argued Gordan.

'I could, but I'm not going to. I'll tell you tonight.'

'All right, miss,' said Mr. Budd. 'If you show us the place, an' this feller's there, you can leave the rest to me.'

'Who is Midnight?' demanded Gordan.

'You'll know tonight — unless anything goes wrong,' she replied.

'What do you mean by that?'

'Unless there's any change of plan. If there is, I'll telephone you.'

'How will *you* know if there's a change of plan?'

'I have ways and means of finding out,' she said. 'Now don't ask any more questions.' She drank the remainder of her coffee and got up. 'I must go.'

'We're going, too,' said Gordan.

'Not for five minutes,' said Audrey Smith coolly. 'I'm not giving you the chance of following me. Bye-bye for now — see you tonight.' She smiled, hurried over to the door, and was gone.

'Well,' said Gordan, looking at Mr. Budd, 'what do you make of her?'

'She seems ter me to be a very competent young woman,' grunted Mr. Budd, leaning back in his chair, which stood the strain manfully. 'A very competent young woman.'

'I know all that.' Gordan took out a packet of Players and helped himself to a cigarette. 'What I mean is, what do you think her game is?'

'Seems pretty obvious ter me. She's out to get this feller, Midnight.'

'But why?'

The big man shrugged his broad shoulders. 'There may be a good many reasons. You never can tell. Maybe he's done somethin' to 'er an' she's out for revenge, or maybe it's jealousy.'

'Jealousy?'

'You'd be surprised at the number o' women who've shopped men because they started carryin' on with somebody else.'

'That's ridiculous. You can't imagine a woman like Audrey Smith ever becoming mixed up with a man like Midnight in *that* way.'

'Experience 'as made me capable of imaginin' most thin's. There's no knowin' the type o' men that some o' these women 'ull fall for. I once knew a feller, ugly-lookin' chap with a face like a monkey, an' in every racket that you could think of, who could scarcely write 'is own name, or speak the King's English, who was runnin' round with the daughter of a duke. She was just mad about 'im, an' no one could do anythin' about it. You can't predict what a woman 'ull do — 'alf the time they don't know themselves.'

'Audrey Smith's not that type at all,' said Gordan. 'There's something else behind her queer behaviour.'

'So long as she delivers the goods,' said Mr. Budd with a prodigious yawn, 'what's it matter? We shall find out.' He got up wearily. 'All these disturbed nights are gettin' me down,' he said, shaking his head. 'I must be goin'. There's a whole 'eap o' work to be got through. These fellers who go around murderin' people an' committin' robberies an' thin's don't realize what a lot o' work they let us in for. Sheer selfishness, that's what it is.'

Gordan left him still grumbling outside the tea shop and walked back to his flat. Vicky, her eyes drooping with lack of sleep, was waiting in the sitting-room, a fresh pot of coffee on a tray beside her.

'You ought to have gone to bed,' said Gordan.

'I wanted to hear what that woman wanted,' said Vicky.

He told her. 'And you're not coming,' he ended firmly. 'It's no good pleading or storming or doing anything that you may be contemplating — you're *not* coming with us tonight.'

'Very well, darling,' she said meekly — so meekly that Gordan should have been suspicious. 'I think I'll go to bed now,' she added. 'What are you going to do?'

'I'm going along to the *Clarion*. I'll get a rest this afternoon.'

He kissed her, and not even the vaguest of premonition warned him of all that was to happen before he saw her again.

15

Gordan had every intention of turning in an account of the murder of Beppo Ricardi for the *Clarion*, and then returning to his flat for lunch and a rest, before setting out to meet Mr. Budd and Audrey Smith at Battersea Park station. But it didn't turn out like this at all. To start with, John Tully was not in the best of tempers that morning. He was not satisfied with the bare account of the murder that Gordan put before him, and insisted that he should get an interview with the dead man's landlady.

In company with a staff photographer, Gordan made his way to Soho and spent a great deal of time listening to all of Mrs. Moreno's woes, how difficult it was to make an honest living these days, and the persecution she had suffered all her life from the police. He got some sort of an interview that he thought would satisfy Tully, and several photographs of Mrs.

Moreno and the house. But by this time it was nearly two o'clock.

It was too late to go back to his flat for lunch; and after telephoning Vicky to say that he was detained, he turned into a pub in Wardour Street for a pint of beer and a sandwich before returning to the offices of the *Clarion*. The staff photographer had gone on ahead to develop his pictures, and Gordan was munching his sandwich alone when he happened to glance into the mirror that backed the shelves behind the bar. The public bar was divided from the saloon by a ground-glass partition and it was reflected in the mirror. Standing at one end of the counter, and gloomily staring at a glass of bitter, was Nosey Williams.

Gordan finished his sandwich and the remains of his beer, left the saloon bar, and hurried round to the public bar.

Williams looked round quickly as he entered, and the gloom on his thin face changed to an expression of alarm and consternation.

'Hello, Nosey,' said Gordan. 'I've been looking for you everywhere. Where have you been hiding yourself?'

The little man regarded him with anything but pleasure. 'I've bin away down in the country,' he muttered uneasily.

'What for? Taking a holiday?'

'Yes, that's it, Mr. Cross,' said Williams quickly. 'I'm goin' back again this afternoon — just come up to do a bit o' business.'

'And what part of the country have you been rusticating in?'

Williams hesitated. His eyes flickered round the bar. 'Osterley,' he said suddenly.

'Why don't you tell the truth, Nosey?'

'What do yer mean?'

'You've just seen Osterley on that advertisement for beer over there. You were trying to think of some place when you saw that.'

'You're wrong, Mr. Cross,' said Williams earnestly. 'I've been in the country — straight I 'ave!'

'You're lying,' said Gordan without heat. 'You've been hiding up. What's scared you? Mr. Midnight?'

Nosey Williams's pasty face went a shade paler. 'No — no,' he stammered.

'You know, I was wrong about that. Some of the boys was pullin' my leg. There ain't such a person, Mr. Cross.'

'You *are* scared, aren't you? You'll have to think of something better than that, though.'

'I'm tellin' yer the truth, Mr. Cross. They was havin' a joke on me.'

'Who's 'they'?'

'Some o' the boys. You wouldn't know 'em.'

'No — and neither would you. There's nothing funny about Mr. Midnight, and you know that as well as I do. Something's frightened you, and you're trying to hedge. If this was all a joke, why did you sent me to The Yellow Orchid that night, and to that bungalow on the river? Was that part of the joke?'

Williams licked his lips. He was looking uncomfortable and uneasy. 'No,' he muttered. He moved nearer, and when he spoke again it was in so low a tone that Gordan had difficulty hearing what he said. 'I don't want ter 'ave nothin' more to do with it. You forced me into it at the start. I didn't want ter get mixed up with it, I told yer that. You put the black on me over Lew Steiner.'

'That's not a nice way of putting it, Nosey,' remonstrated Gordan.

'Nice or not, it's the truth. I wouldn't 'ave 'ad nothin' ter do with it if you 'adn't threatened ter — ' He broke off suddenly, staring beyond Gordan in the direction of the door. Somebody had entered the bar. Gordan looked round to see who it was and found himself face to face with Mr. Patrella.

The man looked a little startled, but he quickly recovered himself and smiled blandly. 'Mr. Cross,' he exclaimed. 'This is an unexpected pleasure.'

There was no pleasure in his eyes. They were hard and wary. He took no notice at all of Nosey Williams, yet Gordan would have been willing to swear it was the little nose he had come there to meet. 'I should hardly have expected you to frequent the public bar, Mr. Patrella,' he said.

'I am — what you call it? — democratic,' answered Patrella easily. 'I am, too, interested in types. I find, sometimes, unusual people in the public bar.'

His eyes slid round towards the embarrassed Williams, but there was no sign of recognition in them. The little man shuffled uneasily. 'I must be goin', Mr. Cross,' he muttered. He reached across to the bar and set down his empty glass.

'I hope you enjoy the rest of your holiday,' said Gordan.

'You are on 'oliday?' remarked Patrella. 'That is a nice thing to be, yes? I wish I were on 'oliday. It is pleasant to forget business and enjoy yourself.'

Nosey Williams hardly looked as though he were enjoying himself. The usual unwholesome colour of his face was even more marked. It was a greyish putty colour, and his eyes were restless. He muttered something inaudible and sidled towards the door.

'You will 'ave a leetle drink before you go?' said Mr. Patrella. 'What is it you drink?'

'No, no, thank yer,' said Nosey Williams, shaking his head. 'I ain't got time . . . got ter catch me train.' He nodded quickly and shuffled out.

'You will 'ave a drink, yes?' invited Patrella. Gordan agreed, and Patrella ordered a pint of beer and a large Haig. 'Your friend — he seem to be a leetle upset,' he remarked.

'Perhaps he has good cause,' said Gordan.

The other shrugged his shoulders. 'You would know more about that than me,' he said. 'Did you enjoy your evening at The Yellow Orchid last night?'

'It was quite pleasant,' answered Gordan, 'except for the sequel.'

'The sequel?' Patrella wrinkled his brows and shook his head. 'I do not understand. What do you mean by the sequel?'

'Do you know the new waiter who was there last night?'

'The new waiter?' Mr. Patrella's expression was even more puzzled. 'Was there a new waiter? I did not notice eem.'

'A man named Beppo Ricardi,' said Gordan, watching him intently. 'He was wearing a very fine Intaglio ring.'

'I did not notice eem,' repeated Patrella. 'These waiters, they come an' they go.' He made an expressive gesture with his hands.

'It's a pity you didn't notice him,' said Gordan. 'He was murdered last night

— stabbed in the back, and his body doubled up and put in my car!'

'Murdered . . . But how terrible!' exclaimed Patrella. He took a quick gulp at his whisky. 'And you found the — the body in your car? What a dreadful thing! Who could have done it?'

'That's what the police would like to know. I was wondering if you might not be able to help.'

'Me!' said Patrella with great surprise. ''Ow could I help? I did not even know this man — what did you say ees name was?'

'Beppo Ricardi.'

Patrella shook his head emphatically. 'I know nothing. I did not know 'e was dead. It ees terrible.'

'Yes — not a very healthy place, The Yellow Orchid, is it?' said Gordan. 'Myra Destry, Laddie Castell, and this man Ricardi.'

'Eet is terrible, terrible. You think it ees someone at The Yellow Orchid who kill these people?'

'What do *you* think?'

'I do not think. I know nothing about it

at all. I go to The Yellow Orchid, after my business is done, for relaxation — that ees all. If these terrible things 'appen, I do not know about them. Why should these people 'ave been killed? I do not know. Perhaps they were mixed up in somet'ing they should not 'ave been mixed up in, but it ees no concern of mine. I am not mixed up in things I should not be!' He swallowed the remainder of his whisky and put down the glass. 'I must go,' he said, looking at his watch. 'I 'ave an appointment that is important. Goodbye, Mr. Cross. Please to give my respects to your so charming wife.'

He smiled, waved his hand, and was gone. Gordan lit a cigarette and thoughtfully sipped the remainder of his beer. Patrella had come to meet Nosey Williams — that was pretty certain — and when he had found that the little man was with Cross, he had pretended not to know him. And Williams had done the same. Gordan was convinced that they both knew each other quite well. There had been no mistaking the flicker of recognition in Williams's eyes when

211

Patrella had come in. There had been apprehension too. The little informer was frightened — he had admitted that he didn't want to have anything more to do with the Midnight business. Gordan had forced him into it in the first place against his will. That night in The Blue Feathers when Sir Franklin Marsh had come into the bar while they had been talking, Williams had been scared. He knew just what kind of people Mr. Midnight had gathered round him.

Gordan remembered what had happened to Myra Destry, Laddie Castell, and the waiter, Beppo Ricardi, and he thought that Nosey Williams's terror was justified.

★　★　★

A combination of circumstances prevented Gordan from being able to get back to his flat before it was time for him to meet Mr. Budd and Audrey Smith at Battersea Park station that night. By the time he had written up the interview with Mrs. Moreno into two sensational columns, John Tully had decided that he wanted someone to go and report a smash-and-grab raid that had taken place in North London. There were no reporters available except Gordan, and when he protested, Tully had snarled: 'You're crime reporter on this newspaper, and this smash-and-grab's a crime. You'll go — and turn me in something worth printing. It'll be a pleasant change!'

Gordan went. He spent the greater part of the afternoon gathering particulars of the raid, which was a very ordinary job. A car had drawn up outside a small jeweller's shop; a man had got out, heaved a brick through the window, snatched a tray of rings, and escaped, dropping most of his booty on the pavement as he dashed for the car. There was nothing very exciting about it. It could have been handled by any junior reporter, and Gordan, thoroughly tired after his broken night's rest, cursed Tully for giving him the assignment.

He telephoned an account of the robbery to the *Clarion* offices at five-thirty, and turned into a little tea shop for a cup of tea. He was planning to go back to his flat for a rest before setting out to meet Mr. Budd and Audrey Smith, but coming out of the tea shop, he ran into an old friend whom he hadn't seen for nearly a year.

Bill Kennedy had been sent abroad for the *Megaphone* to gather news in the Near East, and this was his first leave. He insisted on carting Gordan off for a drink and a chat over old times, and by the time they had consumed several beers and swapped yarns, it was too late to think of going back to Bloomsbury.

Gordan, having got rid of Bill Kennedy with the greatest difficulty, tried to telephone Vicky. But there was no reply, and he concluded that she must have gone out. There was now very little time for him to get to the appointed meeting place, but he managed to find a taxi and reached Battersea Park station three minutes late.

Mr. Budd and Audrey Smith were waiting in the gloomy entrance. 'Thought you wasn't comin'', grunted the superintendent when Gordan joined them. 'She won't tell me nothin'.' He jerked his head irritably towards the woman.

'I didn't want to have to go over it twice, said Audrey Smith. 'I was quite sure Mr. Cross wouldn't fail to turn up.'

'Well, now 'e's 'ere,' said Mr. Budd, 'let's get busy. Where's this feller, Mr. Midnight, goin' to be?'

'On a barge,' answered Audrey. 'It's moored almost opposite the power station and is called *The William Orange*. Did you bring any men with you?'

'There's a carload waitin' round the corner in a side street,' said Mr. Budd impatiently. 'I wish you'd mentioned that it was a barge we was goin' to — I'd 'ave got the river p'lice in on it.'

'There's plenty of time to do that now,' said Gordan. 'Is this barge moored to the bank?'

'No,' Audrey answered. 'In midstream. But there are plenty of small boats tied up to a wharf almost opposite the mooring.'

'We'll get a p'lice launch,' declared Mr. Budd. 'When will this feller arrive?'

'Not before twelve. There'll be plenty of time to make all your arrangements.'

'Will there be anybody on the barge before then?' asked Gordan.

'I don't know. I should think it quite likely that there would be someone.'

'We won't take any risks,' grunted Mr. Budd. 'I'll get on to the river section an' arrange for a big launch ter pick us up further up the river. We can all get in that, includin' the men I brought with me, an' cruise slowly downstream until we come in sight o' this barge. Then we'll lie up in the shadows an' wait till we're sure this feller's on board the barge, an' come in alongside. If he's there, we'll get him.'

There was a public telephone in the station entrance, and Mr. Budd put through his call to the river police. When he rejoined them, his arrangements were complete. A police launch would be waiting to pick them up at Copeland's Wharf on the Surrey side of the river in half an hour. It was possible, apparently, to reach the wharf through a narrow alley without going through the warehouse it served, and for this reason it had been chosen.

It was a damp, raw night with a thin mist that was thicker near the river. Mr. Budd had brought two police cars — one containing the men he had mentioned and a second one for themselves, Sergeant Leek, and a police driver. They had plenty of time, and they took the short journey to Copeland's Wharf easily. As it was, they reached their destination too early. Sergeant Leek, sent down the narrow passage to investigate, returned to report that no police launch had yet put in an appearance.

They waited in the car, Gordan beginning to feel an increasing tingle of excitement. Audrey Smith seemed to be as cool as ever. She sat, pressed up in one corner of the seat, smoking a cigarette and saying nothing. How *did* she come into this business? he thought. Where had she obtained her information that Mr. Midnight would be on the barge that night? Was it first-hand information, or had she obtained it from hearsay? And was it authentic? Would the night end in another disappointment, or would they at last come face to face with the man who was called Mr. Midnight?

Gordan's thoughts were interrupted by the third appearance of the gloomy Leek at the window of the car.

'It's 'ere,' said the sergeant, and he sneezed violently.

'Come on,' grunted Mr. Budd, heaving his massive bulk out of the car.

'I think I'd better stay 'ere,' said Leek. 'There's a thickness in me 'ead.'

'You always 'ad a thick 'ead!' snarled Mr. Budd crossly. 'If you're thinkin' of 'avin' a nice cosy little sleep while we do all the work, you can think again.'

'It wasn't that,' declared the sergeant aggrievedly. 'I was only tryin' ter save meself from gettin' laid up with a cold. What use would I be then?'

'What use are you, anyway?' snapped his superior. 'You come along with us, an' stop moanin'.'

The lean sergeant sighed, but he refrained from further argument and followed them down the passage to the wharf. It was very narrow and very dark, and it sloped steeply. There was a strong smell of rotten wood, mildewed grain, tar and the tang of the river. The surface was uneven, and twice Gordan prevented Audrey Smith from falling. When they came out onto the wharf, they saw that a large launch had put in and was being held by men with boat-hooks to the crumbling landing-stage.

Mr. Budd introduced himself to the inspector in charge and they climbed aboard. The superintendent had brought six men with him, and, although the launch was a big one, they found it was a tight squeeze to find room for everybody.

'You'd better remove the identification lights,' said Mr. Budd before they cast off. 'We don't want to advertise the fact that this is a p'lice boat.'

The inspector gave orders and this was done. The launch moved slowly away from the wharf into midstream, and headed gently downriver.

'You know this barge when we come up with it?' asked Mr. Budd; and Audrey, to whom he had addressed the question, nodded. 'Then you'd better get next the feller at the wheel. You can tell 'im when ter stop.'

The mist was thickening. Both shores of the river were only dark smudges, with here and there the cold glare of an arc light. Before them they could dimly make out the huge bulk of the Lott's Road power station, although it was still some distance ahead. Distances on the river at night could be deceiving. Slowly they crept downstream, the soft chug-chug of the engine scarcely audible. They passed a line of moored barges, and nearer to the shore, several tugs. A clock somewhere in the distance struck eleven.

To Gordan Cross, this trip down the river in the murky gloom was eerie and mysterious. Bulky shapes that looked solid dissolved into shadows, and shadows turned out to be solid. Nothing looked real. They seemed to be moving in a world of dreams, queerly distorted and fanciful; a fairy-tale world where anything might happen.

'There,' he heard Audrey whisper suddenly, 'just ahead on your left.'

Peering through the mist, he made out the vague shape of a barge.

'You're sure that's the one, miss?' asked Mr. Budd.

'Yes, that's it,' she answered without hesitation.

'Go past it on the port side,' said the inspector to the helmsman. 'And keep going on. I'll tell you when to turn.'

The launch went slowly past the dark bulk of the barge. It was a large barge; even in that uncertain gloom, Gordan could make out its size. It floated high in the water, towering above them as they went by, and moored to a bobbing buoy. There was no sign of life on it. If there was anyone on the lookout, they were well hidden. They passed it and left it behind, a smudge on the dark water.

'Keep on until you get to Latham's Wharf,' said the inspector. 'Then turn and come back, keeping well in to the Surrey shore. We can lay up in the shadow of that tug.'

'O.K., sir,' said the man at the wheel.

The launch went on. It seemed to Gordan an interminable time before they swung round in a wide arc and began to head upstream, nosing into the Surrey shore. The tug the inspector mentioned was moored against a wharf almost opposite the barge. They drew into its protecting shadow, the engine ceased its chugging, and they came to a gentle stop, bumping softly against the side of the tug. Two men with boat-hooks, stern and aft, caught the gunwale of the tug and held the launch fast.

'Now all we can do is ter wait,' remarked Mr. Budd. 'I think we're pretty safely hidden 'ere.'

'It'd need a pretty sharp pair of eyes to spot us,' said the inspector. 'I take it that — ' He was interrupted by a prodigious sneeze.

Mr. Budd swung round on Leek. 'Must you do that?' he snarled. 'Couldn't you bang a drum, or fire a few rockets, or do somethin' equally certain to give us away?'

'I'm sorry,' gasped the sergeant. 'I couldn't 'elp it. I've got cold.'

'You'll get it 'ot if yer do that again,' said Mr. Budd. He turned to Audrey. ''Ow do you s'pose this feller 'ull come?' he asked.

'By boat,' she answered.

'I know that,' said the big man a little impatiently. 'But what sort o' boat?'

'I don't know. It's mostly likely to be a

skiff or a dinghy — something silent.'

The inspector uttered a sudden exclamation. He had been scanning the river through his night-glasses.

'What is it?' snapped Mr. Budd.

'There's something moving on the barge.'

16

Mr. Budd took the night-glasses from his hand and peered through them at the dark bulk of the barge, adjusting the focus to his sight. At first he could see no sign of life, and then he made out a little moving blob of shadow near the stern. It looked like the head and shoulders of a man.

'There's definitely someone on the barge,' he said. 'Seems ter be keepin' a lookout.'

'That's what I thought,' agreed the inspector.

'He must have been there all the time,' remarked Gordan. 'Do you think he spotted us?'

'No,' grunted Mr. Budd. 'I can see 'im a bit clearer now. 'E's not lookin' in this direction at all. I don't quite know what 'e's doin'. 'E seems ter be peerin' over the side.'

'Let me have a look,' said Gordan.

Mr. Budd relinquished the glasses, and the reporter put them to his eyes. As he twisted the focusing adjustment, the barge suddenly appeared to loom up with startling nearness. It was as though he had miraculously been transported to within a few feet of it.

There *was* a man near the stern. He was leaning over the side and staring down into the water. After a moment, he straightened up and disappeared from view. Gordan kept the glasses trained on the spot where he had last seen him, and presently he reappeared. It looked as if he had brought something with him from the interior of the barge; something that was rather heavy and bulky, to judge from his movements. He was stooping over it, and Gordan could faintly hear the clank and rattle of a chain.

'Do you think it's this feller we're after?' said Mr. Budd.

'Mr. Midnight?' asked Audrey. 'No, it's too early for him — it's barely half-past eleven. He won't get here before twelve.'

'What's that feller on the barge doin'?' asked the big man. 'Can you see 'im?'

'Yes — he's doing something with a chain,' answered Gordan. 'Attaching it to something, I think.'

'Give me them glasses,' said Mr. Budd, and he almost snatched them from Gordan's hand. 'I can't see 'im at all now,' he grunted a few seconds later. 'Oh, yes, there 'e is. 'E's pullin' at something.' He was silent for a little while, peering intently through the glasses. 'What the 'ell's 'e doin'?' he muttered. 'What's 'e got on the deck there?'

'Perhaps the moorings were coming loose,' suggested Gordan. 'He was doing something with a chain.'

'Well, whatever it was, 'e's gone now,' said Mr. Budd, lowering the glasses. 'Who does that barge belong to, miss?'

'I don't know,' she answered.

'D'you mean they're just usin' it for a kind o' meetin'-place?'

'Yes.'

The big man took another look at the barge through the glasses. It was now quite deserted. There was no sign of its occupant. 'Nothin' stirrin' at all,' commented Mr. Budd.

It was very quiet. Only the soft lap of the river as it swirled past the launch, and the faint sound of traffic on the shore, reached their ears. Presently a clock chimed the three-quarters.

'A quarter to twelve,' muttered Gordan. 'We shan't have long to wait now.' His pulse was beating a little more rapidly than normally. In a few minutes, if Audrey Smith were right, the unknown man responsible for the murder of Myra Destry, Laddie Castell, and the unfortunate Beppo Ricardi would come out of the darkness and the mist. They would come face to face with Mr. Midnight.

'Listen!' breathed the inspector suddenly.

They listened, but they could hear nothing.

'What is it?' whispered Mr. Budd.

'There's a boat coming,' said the river man. 'You can hear the oars.'

His ears, trained to pick up such sounds, may have heard them; but Gordan, although he listened intently, could still hear nothing. 'Are you sure?' he asked.

'Yes, sir.' It was the helmsman who answered. 'There's a rowboat of some description coming downstream. You'll 'ear it in a minute.'

And presently they did hear it. The dip-dip of the oars and the faint creak of the rowlocks came steadily nearer. Peering into the misty darkness, they tried to distinguish the boat, but as yet it was invisible.

'What do we do?' whispered the inspector of the river police in a voice that was so low it was barely audible.

'If it's the people we're expectin',' answered Mr. Budd in the same tone, 'we wait until they've gone aboard the barge, an' then we run in alongside.'

The inspector nodded. He moved over and whispered some instructions to the man at the wheel.

The sound of the oars was now plain, and in a little while they made out the dark smudge of the boat as it began to draw near the barge. Mr. Budd focused his glasses on it. It was a large skiff. 'There seem ter be several men in it,' he murmured close to Gordan's ear. 'I can't see clearly enough to count 'em, but the boat's pretty full.'

'Mr. Midnight isn't among them,' said Audrey. 'They're the men he's coming to meet. He'll come later — alone.'

How do you know so much? thought Mr. Budd. *Whatever the outcome of tonight's work, I'm going to keep an eye on you, madam.*

The skiff, under the power of two pairs of oars, drew into the shadow of the barge. After a second or two, during which the big man could see very little of what was going on, the man he had seen before appeared on the deck of the barge and dropped something down to the men in the rowboat. It must have been a rope-ladder, for they presently began swarming over the low gunwale of the barge, one after the other. Mr. Budd counted six of them.

'They're all aboard now,' he reported. 'All we've got ter do is wait for the arrival of Mr. Midnight an' make our swoop.'

They waited, tense and expectant, but nothing happened. The men on the barge had disappeared below, and there was no sign of any other arrival.

'You don't think he's got wind of

something and changed his plans?' muttered Gordan.

Audrey Smith shook her head. 'If he had, the others would have been notified,' she said; but she looked anxious and worried.

'There might not have been time for that,' said Gordan,

As he spoke, the clock in the distance began to chime the quarters.

'If 'e's goin' ter keep up to 'is name, 'e'll 'ave to hurry,' grunted Mr. Budd. 'It's just on midnight.'

He broke off. Coincident with the striking clock came another sound — the splash of oars. Another boat was approaching, this time from the opposite direction.

'Here he comes,' whispered Gordan.

Mr. Budd made no reply. His glasses were levelled on the dim and shadowy barge. He could not make out the shape of the approaching boat, but the sound of the oars was plainly audible. He concluded that the boat itself was concealed from view by the bulk of the barge, therefore it was coming from the other side. Presently the sound of the oars ceased, there was a pause, and then a soft bump as the nose of the boat came in gentle contact with the side of the barge.

The big man lowered his glasses. 'Give 'im a second or two ter get aboard an' then we'll go,' he muttered.

The inspector nodded. He waited for what seemed to Gordan an eternity, but was in reality only a little over a minute, and then he gave a signal to the helmsman. The engine chugged into life, the two men who had been holding the launch to the tug with a boat-hook fore and aft let go, and the police boat began to slip away. Out from the concealing shadow of the tug it went, describing a wide circle. The engine revved up to full speed, and swift as an arrow, the launch darted towards the barge.

A sudden brilliant light cut a swath through the thin mist as the searchlight on the top of the little cabin was switched on. It lit up the barge with merciless clarity, and the empty skiff that swung and bobbed at the end of a rope from the stern.

The man at the wheel, after the

231

momentary burst of speed, shut off the engine and let the launch glide in alongside the barge under its own momentum. The engine was switched on again for a second in reverse, bringing the launch to a halt, and the boat-hooks caught and held it.

'Away you go,' said Mr. Budd to the men he had brought with him. 'I want everybody you find on that barge detained.'

But there was nobody on the barge except Nosey Williams, and he was dead. They found his body lying on the deck near the stern. He had been stabbed, and a rusty chain had been wound round him, obviously preparatory to dropping the body into the river.

★   ★   ★

It was a tired, disappointed, and altogether dispirited trio who in the small hours of that morning sat drinking hot coffee in an all-night cafe near Trafalgar Square. The evening's adventure had proved a fiasco. An examination of the barge had revealed no sign of the man they had come to find, nor of anyone else except the unfortunate Nosey Williams. The six men who had arrived in the skiff, the man who had been on the barge in the first instance, and the person who had arrived in the second boat had all succeeded in making their escape.

'Some'ow or other,' said Mr. Budd gloomily, 'this feller got wind that we was there. 'E took all the others off in 'is boat — we wouldn't see anythin' because the barge was in the way — an' got away while we was gettin' ready to bring the launch up. The noise of our engine would 'ave drowned any sound they made.'

'How did he know?' broke in Audrey Smith. '*How* did he know?'

Mr. Budd looked at her over the top of his coffee cup. Her face was pale and drawn with fatigue, and there was a worried frown between her eyes. 'I don't know, miss,' said the big man slowly, 'but I think it's time you told us everythin' you know. Another murder's been committed.'

'Poor little Williams,' murmured Gordan Cross. 'No wonder he was so scared about getting mixed up in it.' He took out a packet of Players and helped himself to a cigarette. 'I feel partly responsible for his death. I forced him to give me what information he could.'

'Fellers like Williams 'ave ter take risks,' said Mr. Budd. 'They probably warned 'im what was comin' to 'im.'

'And then Patrella saw him with me in that pub. He must have thought it was a prearranged meeting.'

'That was probably it,' Mr. Budd said. 'Don't you worry about it, Mr. Cross. None o' these little squealers are worth worryin' about. They'd sell their own mothers if the price was right. The point is, Williams must 'ave known somethin' pretty damaging to these people.'

'I believe he knew the identity of Mr. Midnight,' said Gordan. 'I've always been sure of it, although he swore that he didn't.'

'I'm pretty sure I know it, too,' said Mr. Budd.

Gordan stared at him. Audrey Smith dropped the spoon with which she had been stirring her coffee, and it fell with a

234

clatter on the marble table top.

'I can't prove it,' went on the big man, shaking his head, 'but there's not much doubt in my mind.'

'Who?' asked Gordan.

'Remember the feller you said came into that pub in Lambeth — that evenin' you was talkin' to Williams? Williams was scared an' almost ran out o' the place.'

'Sir Franklin Marsh.'

'No!' The almost passionate negative came from Audrey. 'No — you're wrong, absolutely wrong.'

'Then what's *right*?' broke in Mr. Budd sharply. 'What's right, miss?'

'I don't know,' she answered. 'I only know you're quite wrong about Sir Franklin Marsh.'

'If you don't know who this feller Midnight is, I don't see how you can be so certain,' said Mr. Budd. He leaned forward across the table. 'Look 'ere, miss — why don't you tell me 'ow you come to be mixed up in this business? You want ter get this feller caught, don't you?'

'I want to see him hanged!' she retorted, and Gordan was surprised at the venom in her voice.

'An' so do I,' said Mr. Budd. 'We're both tryin' to reach the same result, so why not join forces? You tell me all you know, an' — '

'I can't,' she interrupted, shaking her head. 'If I could, I would. I'll help you all I can, but it must be in my own way.'

'I s'pose you realize the danger?' said the big man seriously.

'You mean you could have me arrested?'

'I mean . . . you've seen what 'appened to Nosey Williams.'

'Oh.' She shrugged her shoulders. 'You needn't worry — nothing like that is likely to happen to me.'

'If these people suspected that you were working against them,' said Gordan, 'you can't tell what they might do.'

'They won't suspect. They know nothing about me.'

'Oh, well,' said Mr. Budd, with a sigh, 'if you insist on bein' mysterious . . . '

'I'm not just trying to be mysterious,' she said quickly. 'Please believe that. I can't do anything else. One day, soon I hope, I'll be able to explain, and then you'll understand.'

'I 'ope I will, miss,' grunted Mr. Budd. He yawned and stretched himself wearily. 'In the meanwhile, 'ow can I get in touch with you in case of emergencies? I'll 'ave to ask you to leave some sort of address.'

She hesitated. Clearly she disliked disclosing anything of the kind. After a minute or two, she fumbled in her handbag, took out a little notebook, wrote something in pencil on one of the leaves, and tore it out. 'This telephone number will always find me,' she said, handing it to Mr. Budd. 'If I'm not there, you can leave a message.'

'Is this your telephone number?' he asked.

'No, it isn't,' she replied calmly.

The superintendent folded the slip of paper and put it away in his pocket. 'Well, I s'pose I'll 'ave to be content with that. What I ought to do,' he added grimly, 'is detain you for questionin' and inquiries.'

'It wouldn't do you any good. I shouldn't answer your questions, and I doubt if your inquiries would lead you anywhere.'

'I'm not goin' to,' he said. 'I'm goin' to let you work this in your own way. I've got a hunch that I'm not bein' a fool.'

'You're not,' she declared. 'Sooner or later, I'll deliver Mr. Midnight into your hands. I promise you that.'

'The sooner the better,' said Mr. Budd. He looked at his watch. 'I'm goin',' he said, hoisting himself to his feet. 'I've got to be at the Yard early in the mornin', an' I'd like ter get a bit o' sleep if I can. Don't seem ter get much these days.'

'We'll all go,' said Gordan. 'Vicky'll be wondering what's happened to me.'

'I should 'ave thought she'd got used to it by now,' remarked the superintendent, lumbering over to the door. 'I'll drop you at your flat, if you like. Can I drop you anywhere, miss?'

'No, thank you,' said Audrey. 'I'll be all right.'

'If you've any news,' said Gordan as he and Mr. Budd got into the waiting police car, 'give me a ring. You've got my number.'

'I will,' she said.

They watched her as she crossed the

square towards Charing Cross. 'Are you going home to Streatham?' asked Gordan as the car moved off.

Mr. Budd nodded.

'Why do that? I can give you a shake-down on the settee. It'll save you at least a couple of hours.'

Mr. Budd considered this. 'That's very nice of you, Mr. Cross,' he said, after a pause. 'I think I will. There isn't much more o' the night, any'ow.'

The car slid through the deserted streets, and ran up the wide length of Kingsway into Southampton Row. It swung round the corner by the Imperial Hotel, crossed Brunswick Square, and pulled up at the entrance to Gordan's flat.

Mr. Budd got heavily out, dismissed the sleepy police driver, and slowly followed Gordan up the stairs. 'I've got an' idea,' he said as the reporter searched for his key, 'that you've invited me to stay ter give a sort of alibi with Mrs. Cross for you.'

'I expect Vicky is in bed and fast asleep. She won't be worrying about alibis.'

239

He opened the front door and switched on the light in the tiny hall. The sitting-room door was open, and to his surprise, the door of the bedroom was open, too. Vicky wouldn't have gone to bed without shutting it.

Telling the superintendent to go into the sitting-room, Gordan went into the bedroom and pressed down the light switch. The room was empty. The bed was smooth and had not been slept in. Suddenly alarmed, Gordan made a quick search of the entire flat. There was no sign of Vicky. She wasn't there!

17

Gordan faced Mr. Budd in the little sitting-room of his flat, his face pale and worried. 'Where can she have gone?' he said.

'Maybe she went out with some friends?' suggested the big man.

'She wouldn't do that without leaving a note. Anyway, she would have been back before this — it's nearly four o'clock. I don't like it, Budd. There's something wrong.'

The superintendent rubbed his chin. He felt that there was cause for the reporter's uneasiness. 'You don't think she may 'ave taken it into 'er head to go to this place The Yellow Orchid, do you?'

'I shouldn't think so. Not on her own.'

'Well, whatever she did,' remarked Mr. Budd with an effort at consolation, 'she did it of 'er own accord. There's no sign of any violence.'

'I'll try The Yellow Orchid.' Gordan

consulted his note book for the number and went over to the telephone. Just as he was in the act of picking up, the receiver the bell rang. 'That's Vicky, I expect,' he said.

But it wasn't. A man's voice came over the wire — an unknown voice that sounded curiously muffled. 'Is that Mr. Cross?' it inquired; and when Gordan replied in the affirmative: 'I tried to ring you before, but you were out.'

'Who's speaking?' demanded Gordan.

'That doesn't matter. I have a message for you. Listen carefully. Your wife is quite safe. She'll continue to remain so, if you behave sensibly. Drop all further interest in the person called Mr. Midnight. Otherwise, you may cause your wife a great deal of inconvenience — perhaps even worse.'

'Where is she? What have you done with her?'

'She's safe, as I told you. Naturally she's a little upset, but there's nothing for you to worry about — provided you do what we wish.'

'What assurance can you give me that

she'll be all right?' asked Gordan quickly.

'If you're prepared to agree, your wife will be allowed to return to you within the next two hours. But I warn you that if you afterwards continue your inquiries, or take any further active steps in this matter, you'll lose her again. The next time, she will *not* be allowed to return. Is that clear?'

'Yes,' said Gordan huskily.

'You agree?'

'I've no option, have I?'

'I'm glad you see it in that light. You can expect the return of your wife within two hours.' There was a click as the caller hung up his receiver.

Briefly, Gordan explained what had been said to Mr. Budd.

'Give me that phone,' snapped the big man. He almost snatched the receiver from Gordan's hand. Getting through to the exchange, he explained who he was and demanded to know where the call had originated. After a short delay, he got the information he required.

'Call-box in the Strand,' he said, banging the receiver back on its rest disgustedly. 'I might've guessed they wouldn't 'ave been silly enough to use a private number.'

'Do you think they'll keep their word?' asked Gordan anxiously. 'Do you think they'll let Vicky go?'

'Of course they will. There's no point in holdin' on to 'er. They used 'er as a hostage to get you out o' the way. If they don't let 'er come back, they'll defeat their own object.'

'Well, they've got me out of the way. 'I've finished with the whole business from now on. I'm not risking any harm to Vicky.'

'I can't blame you,' said Mr. Budd. 'It was a clever move. Well, it's up to me now, isn't it?'

'You and Audrey Smith.'

'Audrey Smith?' repeated Mr. Budd thoughtfully. 'Audrey Smith . . . Hm. You know, I've got some ideas about that woman.'

'What ideas?'

'I'll let you know when I've sorted 'em out. What about some coffee, Mr. Cross? It don't look as though we're goin' to get any sleep, so we'd better 'ave somethin' to keep us awake. I'd 'ave done better to 'ave gone back to my little place at Streatham, after all.'

Gordan made some coffee, and they sat drinking it and smoking, waiting for Vicky to come home. It was just under two hours before they heard a car stop outside, and pulling aside the curtains, Gordan peered out into the grey morning. Vicky was just getting out of a taxi, and he breathed a sigh of relief that she was apparently unharmed. In spite of Mr. Budd's reassurances, those two hours had been a nightmare of anxiety and doubt.

He heard her footsteps coming quickly up the staircase, stumbling a little in her eagerness, and went to meet her. She greeted him with a gasp of indrawn breath and almost fell into his arms.

'Oh!' she said in a husky whisper. 'Oh Gordan . . . '

'Take it easy.' He slipped an arm round her and helped her the rest of the way up the stairs and into the flat. She sank down on the settee, completely exhausted.

'Are you all right?' asked Gordan anxiously.

She nodded. She looked very pale. 'I'm very cold and tired, and — and a little frightened. Make me a cup of tea, darling, and I'll feel better.'

He went out into the tiny kitchen. The kettle was boiling on the gas stove, and in a few seconds he had made a pot of tea and brought it in to the sitting-room.

Vicky drank the hot tea gratefully. After her second cup, a little colour came back into her pale cheeks, and she began to look more like her normal self. Gordan told her what the caller had said on the telephone.

'I know,' she said. 'They told me.'

'What happened — where did they take you?'

She set down her empty cup. 'Give me a cigarette and I'll tell you.'

★ ★ ★

Just after she had finished her tea, the telephone had rung. She had thought it was Gordan, but the voice that reached her when she picked up the receiver had been a stranger's. It was a man's voice, and he said he was speaking for Mr. Cross from the offices of the *Clarion*. Would she meet Mr. Cross there as soon as she could? He was very busy finishing some work and had asked them to ring her.

'I never doubted for a moment that it was all right,' said Vicky. 'I thought there'd been a change in your plans, or something. I put on my hat and coat and left the flat. There was a taxi standing outside. I thought it had just dropped a fare, and what a bit of luck that it should be there just when I wanted it. I told the driver to take me to the offices of the *Daily Clarion*, and hopped inside.'

'The old trick,' murmured Mr. Budd, shaking his head, 'but it always works.'

'I had no reason to suspect there was anything wrong,' said Vicky. 'We started off quite normally, and then we went down a little side turning I thought was a short cut. It was a narrow street, and there was nobody about except a man who was walking slowly towards us. I didn't take much notice of him until the cab suddenly pulled up when it was on a level with him. He wrenched open the door and got in. I still thought it was a mistake — that he'd imagined the cab to be empty — but the next moment he'd thrust a pistol into my face and told me to keep quiet.'

'What was this man like?' asked Mr. Budd. 'Would you recognize 'im again, Mrs. Cross?'

'I don't think I should,' she said. 'He was very ordinary-looking; a nondescript type. You can see dozens like him anywhere.'

'What happened next?' asked Gordan.

'He told me that if I behaved myself and did as I was told, there was nothing to worry about. I asked him what he was going to do, and he said I should soon see. I was terribly scared, but with the pistol pressing into my side, there was nothing I could do. I was sure that if I'd attempted to scream or attract attention in any way, it would have been the end of me, so I sat tight and waited to see what was going to happen. The cab kept twisting and turning through a maze of side streets, but presently we came out by

Westminster Bridge. We crossed into Waterloo Road, ran along Kennington Road, and stopped in a little side street.

'A car was waiting here, and I was forced to get out of the taxi and get in, the man with the pistol accompanying me. The car moved off, but all the windows were covered, so I could no longer see where we were going. There was a glass partition between the driver and the rear of the car, and it had been covered as well, so that it was like sitting in a pitch-black box. I tried to find out from the man with the pistol where we were going, but I couldn't get anything out of him. The darkness and the uncertainty almost sent me into a panic. I had to clench my hands until the nails hurt me to prevent myself screaming. I hadn't the least idea what it was all about; why I'd been kidnapped like this.'

'Didn't it occur to you that it was something to do with the Midnight business?' said Gordan.

'Not at first. I was much too frightened to try and work out why. We seemed to be in that car for ages — actually, it was just over two hours before we stopped, and I was ordered to get out. It was quite dark by now. We seemed to be somewhere in the country, but all I could see were a lot of trees and bushes and the dark bulk of a house of some kind.

'There were no lights in it, but we'd stopped outside the main entrance, which was reached by a flight of shallow stone steps. The man who had brought me there took me by the arm and led me up these steps to a door. He rapped on it with the butt of his pistol, and the sound echoed inside with the queer hollow sound that you associate with an empty house. The door was opened at once, and I was pushed into a dark hall. It was so dark that I could see nothing, but there was a damp musty smell, and I was quite sure that it was an empty house to which I had been brought.'

'Empty 'ouses seem ter 'ave an attraction for this bunch,' remarked Mr. Budd. 'This is the third we've 'eard about. That place at Barnet, an' the bungalow at Staines.'

'I wonder if this house is also the

property of Sir Franklin Marsh,' said Gordan.

'I don't know who it belonged to,' said Vicky, 'but I should think it had been empty for a very long time. It smelt like that. I was guided across the hall and into some kind of room. I could hear breathing round me, but I couldn't see anything. There were people there in the darkness — I had no idea how many, but the effect was terrifying. And then somebody spoke. It was a queer, muffled, whispering voice, so that you couldn't tell whether it belonged to a man or a woman.

'"I'm sorry to have had to cause you all this trouble and inconvenience,' it said, 'but you must blame your husband, Mrs. Cross.'

'"What's he got do with it?' I asked. 'Who are you, and why have I been brought here?'

'"It doesn't matter who I am,' answered the whispering voice. 'Your husband, Mr. Cross, has been meddling in my business and causing me a great deal of annoyance. I've had you brought here to put a

251

stop to his interference in my affairs. If he agrees to drop all further activities concerning me, you'll be allowed to return to him. If not . . . ' The sentence was left incomplete; there was no mistaking what he meant.

' 'You're Midnight,' I said.

' 'A stupid and melodramatic name given me by a few ignorant people,' said the voice. 'I dislike it, but it's as good a name as any other. As soon as it's possible to get in touch with your husband, he'll be told what's happened to you. On his promise to give up all further inquiries into my business, you'll be able to go. I don't think you need have any fear that he won't give that promise. I also have no fear that, once given, it will not be kept. The consequences to you would be too unfortunate. I'm afraid that until we hear from your husband, you'll have to remain here. I regret that it's more comfortable.'

'That was apparently all he had to say, for the man who held my arm pulled me out of the room and into the hall again. He led me over to the staircase and made me sit down on the stairs, and there we stayed for hours. I was cold and cramped and hungry and still very scared. The man who had brought me stayed with me all the time. I don't think I've ever felt so miserable as during that long wait. It seemed as if it was never going to end.'

'It must have been practically all night,' said Gordan.

'It was,' said his wife feelingly. 'And just imagine what it was like sitting on a dusty staircase in a draughty, smelly, empty house. It was the most horrible experience I've ever had. I did drop off to sleep once or twice, but I was so uncomfortable that it was only for a few minutes. It came to an end at last, however. Somebody came through from the back of the hall and called out, 'All right, you can take her back.' I didn't see who it was, and I was too thankful to bother much. I was taken out to the car, and we sped away on another long drive. Eventually I was put down near Victoria Station, managed to pick up a taxi, and here I am.' She leaned forward as she finished speaking and helped herself to another cigarette.

'It must've been gettin' light when you

left that 'ouse to get in the car, Mrs. Cross,' said Mr. Budd. 'Couldn't you see anythin' that 'ud enable you to recognize it again?'

She shook her head. 'Only that it was quite a large house, and there were a great many trees. I've no idea where it was.'

'And the car,' said the superintendent, 'would you recognize that again?'

'No. It drove away almost before I'd set foot on the pavement. I did try to get the number, but the plate was smeared with mud.'

Mr. Budd sighed. 'Well, there it is,' he said wearily. 'These people seem to 'ave arranged the thin' pretty cleverly.'

'I'm through,' declared Gordan. 'I'm having nothing more to do with it. I shall go down to the *Clarion* and tell J.T. this morning. I'm not risking anything more happening to Vicky.'

'You'll get the sack,' said Vicky.

'There are other papers beside the *Clarion*. Anyway, there's nothing else I can do.'

He broke off as there came a sudden

knock on the front door.

'Who the devil can that be?' he muttered. He went out into the little hall and opened the door. A man almost fell across the threshold. His face was muddy, and there was blood from a wound in his forehead.

'I've . . . got . . . to see you, Mr. Cross,' he mumbled.

It was Richard Destry!

18

The man was obviously badly hurt. Gordan had to support him to prevent him from falling, and even as he slipped an arm round him, Destry went limp. As his head fell back, Gordan saw the condition of his face. It was terribly battered and bruised, and the blood was pouring from an open gash across his forehead, a nasty clean cut that looked as if it had been inflicted with a razor.

'Here, Budd, come and give me a hand,' he called.

'What's the matter?' The superintendent came lumbering through the sitting-room door, closely followed by Vicky. 'Who's that?'

'Destry,' said Gordan. 'He's been horribly beaten up, and he's lost consciousness. Help me get him into the sitting-room.'

Between them, they carried the senseless man into the room and laid him on the settee. Vicky gave a little cry as she saw the condition of his face.

'Not very pretty, is it?' grunted Gordan. 'Can you get something to bathe his face with?'

She nodded and hurried away.

'That's a razor slash,' said Mr. Budd, pointing to the deep wound across the brow. 'This must 'ave 'appened somewhere quite close to 'ere. He couldn't 'ave got far in that state. I s'pose this is some more of the Midnight lot's work. They keep pretty busy, I must say.'

'Why should they go for Destry?' asked Gordan.

Mr. Budd shrugged his huge shoulders. 'Maybe 'e'll tell us when 'e comes round. They tried to get 'im before, didn't they? At that bungalow.'

Vicky came in quickly with a bowl of warm water, some lint and bandages. She set them down on the little table beside the settee, and Gordan began to bathe Destry's face gently. He looked a little better when the blood and mud had been removed, but it was impossible to stop the cut from bleeding. Gordan managed, however, to staunch it a little by tying a

257

thick pad of lint over it.

'That'll have to have stitches put in it before it will heal,' he said. 'Those clean edges will never knit together otherwise.'

'Nasty thin's, razors,' remarked Mr. Budd. 'I've seen some 'orrible sights in my time. I remember once . . .'

'I don't think we want any more horrors,' broke in Vicky with a shiver. 'We've got quite enough to be going on with. Don't you think you ought to send for a doctor, Gordan?'

'I suppose we ought,' agreed Gordan; and at that moment Destry stirred slightly and uttered a low moan. 'He's coming round.'

The closed eyes twitched and the lids flickered; the brow drew together in a frown of pain, and Destry's head moved restlessly on the cushion which supported it. His lips parted slightly, as though he were trying to say something, but no sound escaped them. And then suddenly, like the release of a spring-shutter, his eyes opened. He uttered a queer little strangled cry, and tried to struggle up.

'Keep still,' said Gordan, gently pushing

him back on the cushion. 'You're all right.'

The look of panic faded from the man's eyes, and he sank back with a sigh. 'My head,' he whispered feebly. 'My head . . . hurts . . . '

'Would you like some coffee?' asked Vicky, bending down over the settee.

'Yes . . . yes, please,' said Destry. His lips were so puffed and bruised that he had difficulty forming his words.

Vicky went out into the kitchen to make the coffee, and Destry's eyes followed her to the door. When she had gone, they turned back to Gordan.

'Do you feel better?' asked the reporter.

'Yes . . . a little,' answered Destry. 'What . . . happened? Did I . . . pass out?'

'You did,' said Gordan. 'Almost directly after I opened the door.'

'I never thought I'd . . . make it.' Destry raised his hand and touched the bandage round his head. 'They had razors.'

'Who were they? What happened?' asked Gordan.

'There . . . were three of them,' murmured Destry weakly. 'I was . . . on my way here.' He moved his head and winced.

They saw his eyes cloud with pain.

'Don't rush it,' said Gordan. 'You've had a pretty bad time. Take it easy for a bit. You can tell us all about it after you've had some coffee.'

'I'm afraid I . . . still feel a bit . . . rotten. They had knuckle-dusters as well as razors.'

'A reg'lar bunch o' thugs from the sound of it,' remarked Mr. Budd. 'I s'pose they was employed by this feller Midnight?'

'Yes . . . yes,' said Destry with difficulty. 'It must . . . have been Midnight.'

'What's 'e got against you?' asked the big man. ''E tried to get you that night at the bungalow, didn't 'e?'

'Yes.' Destry's voice was a little stronger. 'Yes . . . he tried to get me then.'

'Why?' asked Gordan.

'Because I know who he is.'

'You know?' said Mr. Budd eagerly.

'Who is Mr. Midnight?' demanded Gordan.

'He's — ' began Destry, and then his eyes suddenly became fixed and glazed with fear. He was looking towards the door, and Mr. Budd and Gordan, who had their backs to it, spun round in alarm. A man stood on the threshold, and there was an automatic pistol in his hand. Gordan's cry of alarmed surprise and the sound of the shot were coincidental. Destry gave a convulsive start, half rose from the settee, and then fell back limply. The man with the pistol turned and fled. They heard Vicky scream and the slam of the front door, followed by rapidly retreating footsteps down the stairs.

With surprising speed for his size and bulk, Mr. Budd was out in the little hall. He tore open the front door and went racing down the stone stairway. A shot came from below, and he heard the bullet smack into the wall near his head. A second shot followed, but it went wide, bringing down a spatter of plaster from the ceiling. As he came out of the entrance to the flats, he saw the man he was pursuing spring into a waiting car, which drove off before he had properly closed the door. The superintendent noted the number and hurried back up the stairs to Gordan's flat. Vicky, her face the colour of chalk, was leaning against the wall in the hall.

'Those shots . . . ' she whispered. 'Are you all right?'

'They missed me,' said Mr. Budd reassuringly. ''Ow's Destry?'

'He's dead,' said Gordan, appearing at the sitting-room door. 'Where did that man go?'

'Jumped into a waitin' car,' grunted Mr. Budd. 'I've got the number. With a bit o' luck, we may get 'im.'

He went quickly to the telephone and called Scotland Yard. He was put through to the Information Room, and held a rapid and staccato conversation with the inspector in charge. By the time he had finished, the other tenant of the flats, alarmed and disturbed by the shots, had gathered on the staircase, demanding to know what the trouble was.

Mr. Budd went out to them, told them briefly what had happened, and sent them all back to their respective homes. He came back, panting and wiping his forehead.

''Ow did that feller get in?' he muttered.

'I must have left the front door ajar when we carried Destry into the sitting-room,' said Gordan. He looked wan and haggard. The anxiety over Vicky and the lack of sleep had reduced him to a state of nervous exhaustion. 'He wouldn't have known that, though.'

'He came to finish the job in any case,' said Mr. Budd. 'Destry knew too much, an' they 'ad to stop 'im talkin'. If the door hadn't been open, they'd 'ave got in some other way. Maybe,' he added, thought-fully, 'it was a good thin' for us the door *was* left open.'

'It was horrible,' whispered Vicky with a shiver. 'I looked out of the kitchen door and there he was!'

'All the squad cars'll be lookin' for a black Daimler numbered XL 1507,' said Mr. Budd. 'They won't get very far.'

'I'll bet the car was stolen,' said Gordan, 'and they'll abandon it before they've *gone* very far.'

'Well, we've done all we can,' said the big man wearily. He went over to the still figure on the settee and bent over it. The bullet had struck Destry just below the bandage. There was very little blood where it had entered, but the exit wound had bled freely. The cushion under the head was soaked with blood.

"'E knew who Mr. Midnight was, an' they killed 'im,' said Mr. Budd very softly. 'The question I'd like to know is — who was Richard Destry?'

★   ★   ★

Later, on that same morning, Mr. Budd had an interview with the assistant commissioner. Colonel Blair, neat and dapper as usual, sat behind his big desk and surveyed the weary superintendent with a frown. His fingers gently rolled a pencil up and down the blotting-pad — a sure sign that all was not well and that he was displeased.

'I realize your difficulties, Superintendent,' he said in the cold, polite manner which always made Mr. Budd go hot under the collar, 'but the fact remains that it's very unsatisfactory — very unsatisfactory indeed. There have been five murders: Myra Destry, Castell, Williams, Ricardi,

264

and this man this morning. All these murders are attributable, you tell me, to some unknown person called Mr. Midnight. Who this person is you have no idea, and in my opinion, no really adequate proof that he exists.'

'There's not much doubt about his existence, sir,' said Mr. Budd a little grimly.

The assistant commissioner made an impatient gesture. 'The only evidence you have is hearsay. You yourself had never heard of him until this reporter mentioned him, and he only got his information from the informer, Williams.'

'That's quite true, sir, but in my opinion there's been plenty of confirmation since. This woman, Smith — '

'Merely hearsay,' interrupted Colonel Blair obstinately.

'An' then there was Destry, sir. 'E was goin' to tell us who Midnight was when 'e was shot. There wasn't much 'earsay about that!'

'Well, let's suppose that such a person *does* exist — I'm by no means convinced that he does, but for the sake of argument we'll suppose it. Who is he? Why did he kill this Myra Destry, the band leader Castell, the waiter Beppo Ricardi, Williams, and this man Destry?'

'Because they knew somethin',' said Mr. Budd.

'It sounds very far-fetched to me,' grunted Colonel Blair, shaking his grey head. 'You ought to know by now, Superintendent, that these master criminals don't exist in real life. They only appear in books and sensational newspaper reports.'

'This man isn't a master crim'nal, sir,' said Mr. Budd patiently. ''E's a fence. 'E buys stolen property.'

'There is no need to explain to me the meaning of the word *fence*,' interrupted Colonel Blair coldly.

'I didn't mean that, sir,' said Mr. Budd hastily. 'What I meant was that this fellow they call Mr. Midnight runs a sort o' central clearin' 'ouse for stolen stuff. If a lorry-load o' cigarettes is knocked off, the thieves know they can sell the goods to Midnight — an' the same with anythin' else. 'E doesn't control a gang or anythin' like that, an' 'e doesn't plan the robberies.

266

'E just waits for the little crooks to pinch somethin' an' then buys it from 'em.'

'If you know all this, Superintendent, why hasn't he been caught?'

'Because 'e's clever.'

Colonel Blair frowned. His hand went up and delicately stroked the back of his immaculate head. 'I was under the impression that there were a few clever people in the Criminal Investigation Department,' he said. 'I've always supposed that you were among them, Superintendent. I should be sorry to have to change that opinion.' He leaned forward suddenly and fixed his rather piercing eyes on the unhappy Mr. Budd. 'This is the position,' he said. 'The person or persons responsible for these murders must be found, and at once. I'll give you a week. If at the end of that period you can't report some definite progress, the case will have to be given to someone else. That is all.'

Mr. Budd left the office in anything but a pleasant frame of mind. When Colonel Blair took it into his head to be nasty, he could be very nasty indeed. The superintendent lumbered back to his own cheerless little room to seek solace in one of his evil-smelling black cigars.

There was no sign of Leek. The activities of the night had apparently proved too much for him. *Probably overslept*, thought Mr. Budd irritably as he wedged himself in the chair behind his desk and lighted a cigar. He was feeling very tired himself. There was a dull ache in his head and his eyes burned. He closed them and began to think.

There was some reason for the assistant commissioner's complaint. The whole case had been very unsatisfactory — clues that led nowhere; situations that had started out to be promising only to prove disappointing. Twice he had been hoping to catch the elusive Mr. Midnight red-handed, as you might say, and failed at the last moment. And now it looked as though it might be even more difficult.

There was no more help forthcoming from Gordan Cross. The reporter had made it quite clear that he was through. He wasn't risking anything happening to his wife, and you couldn't blame him. Nor would there be any more information from poor little Nosey Williams. He had suffered the penalty for his inquisitiveness.

There might be a chance of getting something out of Audrey Smith, but that depended on her. And there was still Mrs. Destry, with the same name as the woman who had been murdered at the house in Barnet. They had tried to get in touch with her to inform her of her husband's death, but she wasn't at the flat in Evesham Mansions. She had, according to the porter, gone away in a taxi on the previous night and had not yet returned. Where she had gone, the man was unable to say. He thought she might be going to stay with some friends, because she had taken a small suitcase with her; but where she had gone or for how long was unknown.

Maybe, thought Mr. Budd, *the newspaper reports of her husband's death will bring her back. But will she be able to tell us anything, if they do?* A search of the flat had revealed nothing to show what connection Richard Destry had with the affair. What *was* his connection?

One thing was certain: unless he wanted this to be written against his name as a failure, he would have to do something pretty quickly. A week, Colonel Blair had given him. Mr. Budd shook his head. It wasn't long. He was no nearer to finding Midnight than he had been at the beginning. A week.

He must have dozed for a moment or two, because he never heard Sergeant Leek come in. When he opened his eyes, it was to see the melancholy sergeant standing uncertainly just inside the door.

'Oh, it's you, is it,' grunted Mr. Budd. 'I thought you'd resigned.'

'I'm sorry I'm late,' mumbled Leek. 'I think I must 'ave caught a chill on the river last night. My 'ead was so thick when I woke up . . . '

'That's just its natural state,' growled his superior. 'You're lucky to 'ave woke up. I 'aven't been to sleep.'

'You was asleep when I came in,' said the lean sergeant tactlessly.

'I was deep in thought.'

'You was snoring,' declared Leek. 'I could 'ear you as I came up the passage.'

'Maybe I did drop off fer a second or two,' admitted Mr. Budd, 'but it was no longer. I've been on the go all night, not like some people I could name.'

'If you mean me,' said Leek in an injured tone, 'I scarcely slept a wink. I was tossin' an' turnin' most o' the night.'

'Guilty conscience, I s'pose. I wonder you don't blush every time you draw yer pay. I s'pose, after all these years, you've got 'ardened.'

'I work for my money,' said Leek indignantly.

'You must 'ave got a sideline.'

'Anyway, there's no 'arm in gettin' a bit o' rest when you can. There was nothin' happenin'.'

'Oh, no,' said Mr. Budd sarcastically. 'Nothin' 'appenin' at all! Only Mrs. Cross was kidnapped, and Destry was beaten up an' murdered. It's been a wonderfully quiet night!'

Leek stared at him. His jaw dropped open, making his long face appear longer. 'You don't mean it?' he gasped.

'Of course I don't,' snarled Mr. Budd. 'I'm goin' in for writin' sensational novels, an' I'm tryin' out the plot on you!'

'There's no need to get like that. 'Ow was I ter know about all this?'

'Too busy tossin' an' turnin' in your comfortable bed ter know about anythin', eh? If you took an interest in your job, like me, you wouldn't 'ave to be told about these thin's. You'd be there on the spot when they 'appened.'

''Ow did *you* come to be on the spot? I thought you was goin' home?'

'I put duty before my personal comfort,' said Mr. Budd with great self-righteousness. 'I *was* goin' home, but luckily I called in at Mr. Cross's flat first, an' that's 'ow I came to be on the spot.' He omitted to tell Leek why he had gone to Gordan Cross's flat. 'If you can bring yerself to take a bit of interest in yer job, I'll tell you what 'appened.'

The sergeant listened while the superintendent acquainted him with the events of the night. 'I seem to 'ave missed a lot,' he commented when Mr. Budd had finished.

'That's nothin' new,' said the superintendent. The telephone bell rang, and he picked up the receiver. 'Hello,' he called. 'Oh, yes . . . yes . . . Right . . . You're quite sure? All right, thank yer for the information.' He banged down the telephone on its rest and struggled out of his chair. 'Come on,' he said, reaching for his hat.

'Where are we goin'?' asked Leek.

'We're goin' to see Sir Franklin Marsh. That car, XL 1507, belongs to 'im.'

19

Sir Franklin Marsh, when he heard what they had come about, disclaimed all knowledge of the use to which his car had been put.

'I can't understand it,' he said, shaking his head. 'That car is one I keep at The Yellow Orchid for emergencies. It was there last night.'

'Well, it was found this mornin' abandoned in a little side street in Camberwell, sir,' said Mr. Budd. 'an' it was used by this gunman when he shot Destry.'

'It must have been stolen. It wasn't in a garage. It used to stand in the car park at the roadhouse.'

'It seems rather peculiar to me that this man should 'ave gone all the way to St. Albans to steal a car 'e wanted to use in Bloomsbury.'

'It does.'

'It's also peculiar,' continued Mr. Budd, 'that the man who was killed should 'ave been a tenant of yours.'

Sir Franklin raised his eyebrows slightly. 'Do you think so?'

'Doesn't it strike you as a strange coincidence, sir, that all these crimes are in some way connected with you? That woman was killed at *your* house in Barnet. Castell's body was found at a bungalow owned by *you*. This man Destry was a tenant of yours, and the man who shot 'im made 'is escape in *your* car.'

'What are you insinuating, Superintendent?' broke in Sir Franklin coldly.

'Nothin', sir,' said Mr. Budd. 'I'm only pointin' out how queer it is that you seem ter be connected with all these thin's.'

'Only in the very slightest degree. I think we went into all this when you called to see me before, and I can see no advantage to be gained by repeating ourselves. I'm afraid I can't spare you any more time now; I have an appointment.'

There was nothing Mr. Budd could do but go. 'That's a pretty cool feller,' he remarked to Leek as they walked along the Embankment. ''E's not givin' anythin' away, an' 'e knows we 'aven't sufficient evidence to do anythin' about it.'

'Maybe 'is car was stolen,' said the sergeant.

'Maybe it wasn't!' retorted Mr. Budd. 'You can't tell me that all them thin's I mentioned was coincidences. They couldn't be. That feller's in this business up to 'is neck, but we can't prove it.'

'Do you think 'e's Midnight, then?'

Mr. Budd pulled at his nose irritably. 'I don't know what to think. Sometimes I do, an' sometimes I don't.'

They walked along for a little way in silence, and then the lean sergeant said, 'It seems a silly thin' to leave so many clues.'

'What do you mean?' demanded the big man.

'Well, if this feller *is* Midnight, why kill these people in places that belong to 'im, an' why use 'is own car for that other feller to make 'is getaway in? It's childish, ain't it? 'E must've known that it could be traced back to 'im.'

'There's somethin' in that,' agreed Mr. Budd; and Leek, who from long experience had expected a scathing reply, was so taken aback that he tripped over the

276

kerb and nearly fell under a passing taxi.

'Can't you walk yet without gettin' them big feet yours tangled up?' snarled the superintendent. 'If I 'adn't grabbed you, you'd 'ave been run over!'

'I didn't see that we'd come to a crossin',' explained flustered sergeant. 'I was thinkin'.'

'That would account fer nothin' 'appenin',' said Mr. Budd rudely, and he spoke no more until they were back in his office at Scotland Yard. When he had squeezed himself into the chair behind his desk and lighted one of his foul cigars, he looked across at Leek. 'You've given me an idea,' he grunted.

The sergeant brightened. 'I 'ave?'

'I know such a thin' sounds utterly ridic'lous, but you 'ave.'

'They come to me sometimes,' said Leek complacently. 'I'll be sittin' doin' nothin', or maybe just walkin' along, an' suddenly I get an inspiration.'

'Now don't go gettin' a swelled 'ead. When I said you'd given me an idea, I didn't mean that you'd solved the ruddy problem. You've just supplied me with a new angle, that's all.'

'P'raps it'll lead to solvin' it?' suggested the sergeant hopefully.

'I'm not so sure about that, but it'll give you a little job o' work to do.'

The brightness fled from Leek's face. His jaw dropped, and he looked at Mr. Budd unhappily. 'Oh!' he murmured in dismay.

'That's what comes of gettin' ideas. Ideas are no good unless you follow 'em up with a lot of 'ard work.'

Leek made a mental decision not to have any more ideas in the future. 'What do you want me to do?' he asked without enthusiasm.

Mr. Budd drew a pad of paper towards him, picked up a pencil, and began to write busily. He wrote for ten minutes, during which the lean sergeant watched him apprehensively. It seemed that the 'little job of work' was likely to be a big one. Leek, who had spent the greater part of his time in the C.I.D. making endless and very often futile inquiries, and in going here, there and everywhere questioning Tom, Dick and Harry and even people with less euphonious names, felt that he had let himself in for another spell of hard foot-slogging drudgery. He was not disillusioned.

'Come over 'ere,' said Mr. Budd, throwing down the pencil and running his eye over what he had written. 'This is what I want you to do. 'Ere's a list o' thin's I want to know.' He jabbed at the paper in front of him with a stubby finger. 'It may take you some time to get the answers ter these questions, an' you'll 'ave to use tact in doin' it, but I've got to 'ave 'em, see?'

Leek saw only too clearly. The list of questions which his superior had prepared was a formidable one. 'It's goin' to take me all me time.'

'Don't worry about that,' said Mr. Budd encouragingly. 'Just remember that every hour is bringin' you nearer to the time when you perpetrate the biggest swindle that's ever been put over on the taxpayers, an' draw yer pension!'

★   ★   ★

All the evening newspapers carried a full account of the murder of Richard Destry. It had been given front-page prominence, and in each instance there was a photograph of Gordan Cross's flat, the room in which the crime had been committed, and a close-up of the settee.

Since the fact of the murder had become known to Fleet Street, the Bloomsbury flat had been besieged by reporters and photographers. Most of them were personally known to Gordan and regarded him with undisguised envy.

'What a chance!' exclaimed Preston of the *Evening Banner*. 'I wish it had happened to me, old man. You'll be able to spread yourself in tomorrow's *Clarion*.'

When Gordan told him that he had no intention of writing a line for the *Clarion* about it, Preston looked at him as though he had gone mad.

'You get the scoop of a lifetime thrown in your lap, and you're not going to . . . ' Words failed him. He stuttered speechlessly.

John Tully was far from speechless when he heard. 'What's the matter with you, Cross?' he almost screamed over the telephone. 'This thing happens in your own flat and you won't write it up! Why, man, it's sensational. I'm keeping two columns on the front page with a turn-over to page three.'

'You'll have to get somebody else to fill 'em, J.T.,' said Gordan.

'You're crime man on this paper, aren't you? Damn it, man, what's the matter with you?'

'I'm having no more to do with this Midnight business.'

'But you were the first to suggest such a person existed. It's unheard of. It's — it's sacrilege.'

'I can't help it. I've made up my mind.'

'It's never been heard of in the whole history of Fleet Street. You call yourself a newspaper man, and you turn down a thing like this? Don't you know that a reporter's first duty is to his paper? Haven't you ever heard of the word 'loyalty'?'

'Look here, J.T. I can't explain, but I'm feeling pretty bad about this.'

'You'll feel worse,' said Tully, almost

incoherent with rage. 'You turn me in a good story on this murder, or you're fired, you understand? Fired!'

'I understand. I'm sorry.'

'I'll make you sorrier,' shouted Tully so loudly that the telephone jarred and crackled. 'I'll see that you never get another job on any newspaper as long as you live. I'll blacklist you wherever the meaning of the word 'news' is known! I'll — '

Gordan didn't hear what else he was going to do. He hung up the receiver.

When the last of the reporters had gone, and they had the flat to themselves, Vicky brought in some tea. She looked very pale, and there were dark shadows under her eyes from lack of sleep. There had been no chance of even the shortest rest. She poured out the tea and gave a cup to Gordan. 'Cheer up, darling,' she said.

'There's not much to be cheerful about, is there?' he said, stirring the tea listlessly. 'I've lost my job, and it doesn't look as though I'd ever be able to get another — not on a newspaper, anyway.'

'You shouldn't have let them scare you.'

'What else could I do? I had to agree to what they demanded to get you back.'

'I know,' she said, 'but you've *got* me back. There's no reason why you should keep to your promise. It was extracted under duress, and even in law that doesn't hold good.'

'I daren't risk it,' said Gordan, shaking his head. 'If I go on with the Midnight business, they'll carry out their threat against you. It's no good saying they can't,' he added quickly as she began a protest. 'You know what happened to Destry.'

'I'm willing to take a chance.'

'I'm not willing to let you. It's no use, Vicky. I've just got to accept the situation.'

'Surely there's some way out,' she said, frowning. 'You can't let your reputation be ruined like this.'

'It's either my reputation or your life. I prefer to sacrifice my reputation.'

'What are we going to live on if Tully sees that you're barred everywhere?' she said practically.

'There's a little money in the bank, and

I suppose I can get some other kind of job.'

'What other kind? You've no training for any other kind. The only jobs that are going these days are jobs for trained men. They wouldn't be any use to you.'

'I might try writing fiction. Tully's influence wouldn't extend to that.'

Vicky helped herself to a cigarette. 'It might take you a long time before you got anything published,' she said. 'And apart from anything else, you *like* your job. You worked hard to get on the *Clarion* as crime reporter.'

'What's the use of going into that, darling? I've lost the job, and that's all there is to it.'

'You wouldn't lose it if you turned in that story. When is the deadline? What's the latest you'd have to turn the copy in to catch the morning edition?'

'Midnight. They might hold the presses back until later, if they know the stuff was coming.'

'Ring up Tully and tell him the stuff *is* coming.'

He shook his head. 'Can't be done,

284

darling. I've told you I won't risk it.'

'You won't have to risk anything. I'm going to be safe enough. I'm going to make it impossible for Mr. Midnight, with all his cleverness, to harm me in any way!'

'How can you make sure of that? If I could be certain that you would be perfectly safe . . . '

'You can,' she replied. 'Get on the phone to Tully.'

'You tell me what you're going to do,' he said suspiciously.

Vicky got up. 'I'm going straight out now,' she said triumphantly, 'and I'm going to smash the window of that jeweller's shop in Kingsway with a hammer, and I'm going to steal a tray of rings.'

'Don't be absurd — '

'It's not absurd. I shall be arrested and locked up in a cell. And if Mr. Midnight or any of his followers can do me any harm *there*, it'll be a miracle!'

20

Mr. Budd heard of Vicky's arrest when he reached the Yard the following morning. Gordan had been waiting impatiently for nearly an hour to tell him all about it. And when he heard, he chuckled until his face grew scarlet and Gordan thought he was going to have an apoplectic fit.

'That's one of the brightest ideas I've 'eard for a long time,' he gasped. 'Mrs. Cross 'ad a brainwave there. Where did they take 'er?'

Gordan told him the name of the police station.

'She'll be safe enough there,' said the superintendent. 'These thugs won't be able to touch 'er. An' I'll see that she's kept there until we get the whole bunch, includin' this Midnight feller, under lock and key.'

'What I thought you might be able to do,' said Gordan, 'is to see that she's made as comfortable as possible.'

'You leave it to me, Mr. Cross,' said Mr. Budd. 'She'll come up before the magistrate this mornin', an' I'll arrange that she's remanded in custody for a week — that should give us long enough. You needn't worry about your wife anymore; the person you've got to worry about now is yourself.'

'I can look after myself,' said Gordan confidently.

'You'll need to,' said Mr. Budd seriously. 'They'll be after you. They'll know just why Mrs. Cross 'as done this, yer know. You'll need to look after yourself very carefully.'

'Is there any further development?'

'No. I've got Leek out makin' one or two inquiries, but they're only to confirm an idea of mine. What I want to do is to get 'old of Mrs. Destry. I was 'opin' that she'd see an account of her 'usband's murder in the evenin' papers.'

'You don't think anything's happened to her as well?'

'I wouldn't like to say. I 'ope it 'asn't, 'cos I'm countin' on her bein' able to tell us a lot. Still, you never can tell. If she don't put in an appearance today, after she's 'ad time to see the morning papers, I shall begin to think somethin' 'as happened to 'er. I read that bit of yours in the *Clarion* while I was 'avin' my breakfast, Mr. Cross. Pretty good, I thought it was.'

A delighted John Tully had also thought it was 'pretty good'. As soon as Vicky had put her ingenious plan into execution and was safely ensconced in the police station under lock and key, Gordan had taken a taxi to the offices of the *Daily Clarion* and made his peace with the irate news editor. He had explained the whole situation to Tully, who had laughed even more heartily than Mr. Budd when he heard of Vicky's way out. Free from anxiety, and content in the knowledge that he still retained his job, Gordan had hammered out the best piece of work of his life on a typewriter in the reporters' room. The account of the murder of Richard Destry which appeared in the columns of the *Clarion* the next morning was sufficient to delight the heart of any news editor anxious to satisfy a sensation-loving public.

'You 'aven't 'eard anythin' more from

that gal, Audrey Smith, I s'pose?' said Mr. Budd.

'No,' replied Gordan. 'I rather expected to after she'd read the papers.'

'Maybe you will. I've got an idea that you will.' He rubbed his chin. 'Between 'er and Mrs. Destry, I'm 'opin' to get to the bottom of this business.'

'I hope we get to the bottom of it soon,' declared Gordan. 'I want to get Vicky out of that cell just as quickly as I possibly can.'

'It wouldn't surprise me if that was sooner than you expect. Do you know what I'm goin' to do, Mr. Cross? I'm goin' to put you under police protection from now on.' He picked up the house telephone at his elbow. 'Put me on to extension 35,' he said.

Gordan tried to dissuade him, but the big man wouldn't listen. As the result of a brief conversation with 'extension 35', there shortly appeared in Mr. Budd's tiny office a large thick-set man who was introduced to Gordan as Detective Sergeant Brill.

'You'll stay with Mr. Cross wherever 'e

goes,' said Mr Budd. 'An' when 'e goes 'ome, you'll go with him. I'll arrange for you to be relieved. You'll do eight hours o' duty an' eight hours off, turn an' turn about with yer relief. Now, I'm makin' you responsible for Mr. Cross's safety, you understand?'

'Yes, sir,' said the stolid Brill.

'Right,' said Mr. Budd, 'you can pick Mr. Cross up when 'e leaves 'ere. In the meanwhile, you'd better get permit to carry a gun. There's every chance you'll need it.'

Gordan took his leave a few minutes later, and when he had gone, Mr. Budd put his feet up on his desk and lapsed into deep thought. He remained so throughout the morning and well into the afternoon, his eyes closed, his hands clasped loosely over his capacious stomach, scarcely moving except to light one of his atrocious cigars.

He was still in the same position when Leek came in. The lean sergeant looked very weary. 'I've got what you want,' he said. 'I 'aven't made a report in writin', but I can tell yer.'

'That'll do,' grunted Mr. Budd. He swung his legs off the desk and sat forward in his chair. 'Go ahead.'

Leek went ahead. For over three-quarters of an hour, he talked while the superintendent made hurried notes on a pad in front of him, interjecting a question every now and again.

'Now we can start the ball rollin',' he remarked, hoisting himself out of his chair. 'an' I've an idea there's goin' to be a lot of fun.'

'What are yer goin' to do?' asked Leek as Mr. Budd lumbered over to the door.

'I'm gettin' a warrant for the arrest of Sir Franklin Marsh,' said Mr. Budd, and he went out, leaving Leek staring at the closed door in blank amazement.

* * *

Sir Franklin Marsh was arrested that evening just as he was leaving his Chelsea house for The Yellow Orchid. He seemed a little dazed at first when the warrant was read to him, but this was quickly replaced by anger.

'This is outrageous!' he stormed. 'I shall institute an action for damages!'

'You can do what you please,' said Mr. Budd calmly. 'At present yer comin' along with us.'

'I demand to be allowed to get in touch with my solicitor.'

'You're entitled to do that if you wish.'

Mr. Snood, a thin yellow-faced man with grey hair and stooping shoulders, was hastily summoned from his private residence. He argued and expostulated, but to no avail. Sir Franklin was whisked away in a police car and charged at the nearest police station.

'You'll hear a great deal more about this,' said Mr. Snood indignantly. 'The whole thing is preposterous — preposterous. I shall advise my client to — '

'Let me advise you,' interrupted the big man, 'not ter do anythin' you may be sorry for.' A remark that reduced the astounded lawyer to speechlessness.

The newspapers splashed the arrest of Sir Franklin Marsh in heavy type on their front pages, and Mr. Budd read the various accounts with satisfaction.

'If you can't justify this arrest,' said Gordan when the superintendent called on him, 'you're going to get into all the trouble in the world.'

'I know,' said Mr. Budd. 'Don't let's worry about that. I came ter tell you that there'll probably be an unexpected development — unexpected so far as you're concerned — an' it'll 'appen 'ere. When it does, get me on the phone at once.'

'What are you expecting to happen?' asked Gordan curiously, but Mr. Budd refused to discuss this. 'There's been no news of Mrs. Destry, has there?' inquired the reporter.

'Not up ter now.'

'It looks bad, doesn't it? I'm afraid they must have got her, too.'

'I think somebody's got her.'

Gordan looked at him suspiciously. 'What are you up to? I believe you know a lot more than you've told me.'

'Do you, now?' remarked Mr. Budd blandly.

'When you start getting mysterious, it usually means that you've practically got everything in the bag.'

'Well, we shall see. We've got Sir Franklin Marsh, any'ow.'

'Do you think he *is* Midnight? Are you quite sure you've got the right man?'

'I'm quite sure I've got the wrong one,' replied Mr. Budd with the greatest complacency.

'Then why in the world have you arrested him?' asked Gordan in astonishment.

'Cheese.'

'Eh?'

'You put cheese in a mousetrap,' explained Mr. Budd carefully.

'What the deuce are you talking about?'

'The mouse comes along and nibbles at the cheese, an' snap goes the trap,' said Mr. Budd. He rubbed his hands together. 'Simple, ain't it?'

'Do you mean that you've arrested Sir Franklin Marsh as a kind of bait — to bring Mr. Midnight into the open?' asked the puzzled reporter.

'No, I don't think it 'ud do that,' answered Mr. Budd, shaking his head.

'Then what in heaven's name *do* you mean?' cried Gordan in exasperation.

'You'll see — at least I 'ope you will. If you don't, I shall 'ave to resign.'

The telephone bell rang at that moment, and Gordan picked up the receiver. It was Audrey Smith. 'I must see you tonight,' she said urgently. 'Will you be in at seven o'clock?'

'Yes,' answered Gordan. 'What — '

'I'll come to your flat,' she interrupted. 'Don't let anything prevent you being in.'

'All right,' he said, 'but I wish you'd — '

'I can't say anything more now,' she broke in quickly. 'Don't forget — seven o'clock tonight.' There was a click as she hung up her receiver.

'I was wonderin' 'ow long it'd be before you 'eard from 'er,' said Mr. Budd when Gordan told him who it was and what she had said.

'Is that what you were expecting to happen?'

'Partly. I'll be 'ere at six-thirty. I've got an idea that tonight is goin' to see the end of this business.'

'I hope you're right. Vicky will be able to come home then. But I wish you'd tell me more about it.'

'I like to 'ave me little mysteries,' said Mr. Budd. 'It puts a spice of romance into the sordid routine o' police work. If I was you,' he added very seriously, 'I wouldn't go out of your flat. Just stay 'ere an' let Brill keep you under 'is eye. We don't want no complications now, an' if you was to get murdered it'd take my mind off other thin's.'

21

It was a quarter past six when Mr. Budd arrived at Gordan Cross's flat and was admitted by the careful Sergeant Brill. 'I'm a bit early,' he said, 'but I thought it was as well ter be on the safe side. It's an 'orrible night.'

It was. The wind had risen almost to gale force, driving before it a thin sleety rain that whipped the face like tiny flails, and it was very cold. Before morning it would be freezing; already thin layers of ice had formed in the gutters. Acting on Mr. Budd's advice, Gordan had remained in the flat, roaming about in alternative moods of depression and excitement. Mr. Budd had arranged that he could telephone Vicky, and this he had done, learning that she was quite comfortable and rather enjoying her experience, though she was a little perturbed at the thought that she might be missing something.

'Well,' remarked Mr. Budd, warming his hands at the gas fire, 'it won't be long now before we know whether my little idea is comin' off or not.'

'Supposing it doesn't?' said Gordan pessimistically.

'Then I'm goin' ter be on the carpet. But I think it will.'

It was exactly seven o'clock when there came a knock at the door. Brill went to answer it, and they heard voices in the tiny hall. A moment later, the stolid sergeant ushered Audrey Smith into the sitting-room. But to Gordan's surprise, she was not alone. She was followed by another woman whom the reporter recognized at once. It was Mrs. Destry. She looked very pale and haggard, and there were traces of recent crying about her eyes.

'I expected you'd be here,' said Audrey Smith as she saw Mr. Budd. 'I'm very glad you are, because we've got quite a lot to tell you.'

'I thought you would 'ave, Miss Marsh,' said Mr. Budd, and Gordan drew in a quick breath. So that was who she was — this woman who called herself Audrey 'Smith'.

'So you know who I am, do you?' she said. 'How did you find out? Did my father tell you?'

Mr. Budd shook his head. 'No, miss. I 'ad a few inquiries made an' discovered that Sir Franklin 'ad a daughter. 'Is wife 'ad died at her birth.'

'How did you know it was me?'

'You might call it a hunch. The daughter's Christian name was Audrey. S'pose you tell us the whole story, miss — you an' Mrs. Destry.'

'That's what we've come for. Why did you arrest my father?'

'I thought it was time thin's was brought to an 'ead,' said Mr. Budd, and his tone was almost apologetic. 'I guessed that would do it.'

'I see — a sprat to catch a mackerel.' She nodded quickly. 'Very clever of you. But supposing your hunch had been wrong?'

'I 'ad to take the risk of that.'

'Look here,' interrupted Gordan, 'I'm all at sea. If you're Sir Franklin Marsh's

299

daughter, why on earth call yourself 'Smith'?'

'You'll understand that when you've heard what I've got to tell you,' said Audrey Marsh. 'My father has never been a rich man — ever since I was a child, we'd been poor. A few years ago he speculated with what little money he did have and lost it. The situation was desperate, and in order to retrieve it, my father committed a criminal act.'

'Ah,' murmured Mr. Budd. 'I thought there was somethin' like that.'

'I'm not going to tell you what it was,' she went on, ignoring the interruption, 'but he would have got a heavy sentence if he'd been found out, with all the attendant disgrace. He was not found out. With the money he . . . acquired, we were able to go and live in a small cottage in the country. He still owed a great deal, but he was hoping that he would be able to keep his creditors quiet until he had found some way of making money. We managed fairly well on the little we had, though it meant cutting everything down to the minimum. And then one morning, a letter came for my father. It seemed to upset him very much. He didn't tell me what it was about, and I thought one of his creditors was getting nasty.

'The following day he went up to London, making the excuse that he had a business appointment. When he came back, I could see he was terribly worried. I asked him if there was anything the matter, and he said no, but I was quite sure that he wasn't telling me the truth.' She paused, took a cigarette out of her bag, and lighted it.

'From this time on,' she continued, 'everything changed. Instead of being poor, my father suddenly became rich. He started buying property, a car, all sorts of things that he could never have afforded before. I was bewildered and worried. I couldn't understand where this money was coming from, and he refused to offer any explanation. I could see that he was very worried, too, and it made me horribly apprehensive and uneasy. One day he told me that he'd bought a house in Chelsea and proposed to go and live there.

' 'I think you'd better stay on here, Audrey,' he said. 'In case of any trouble, you'll be out of it all.' I begged him to tell me what trouble he expected, and where he was getting all this money from. 'It isn't mine,' he said. 'I'm only acting as a kind of agent for somebody else.' I asked him who he was acting for, and he shook his head. 'I don't know,' he said, and then he told me the whole story.'

'Blackmail?' said Mr. Budd softly.

She nodded. 'Somebody had discovered what he'd done, and this person held the proof. The letter he'd received that morning had made an appointment for him to see this man and consider a proposition.'

'Then 'e did know who it was?' interjected the big man eagerly.

'No. The interview took place in a completely dark room in that empty house in Barnet. My father never saw who he was talking to, and the man never spoke above a whisper.'

'Takin' no chances,' grunted Mr. Budd. 'Go on, miss.'

'I expect you've guessed what the proposition was that was put up to my father,' she said. 'This man was in possession of a lot of money he wanted to invest. It was essential, however, that the investments should not appear to be his. They were all to be made in my father's name, and he was to receive a percentage on every deal. The man hinted that if he refused, the proof of what my father had done would be sent to the police. In plain words, my father was to do exactly what he was told or face the consequences.'

'That's where the money came from to start The Yellow Orchid?' asked Gordan.

'And to buy Evesham Mansions,' she answered. 'Outwardly, all these things belonged to my father; actually they were the property of this unknown person.'

'Our friend, Mr. Midnight.'

'Yes — my father didn't realize that for a long time. When he did, he was horrified.'

'How did he find out?' asked Gordan.

Audrey Marsh nodded towards Mrs. Destry, who had been sitting silently listening. 'They discovered it,' she said. 'Mrs. Destry and her husband. I was very worried about my father. I was terribly afraid that sooner or later he would get into serious trouble. If there was any trouble, he'd have to take all the blame, because nobody would believe the truth — it was too fantastic. There was only one way to safeguard him, and that was to find out who the person was who was employing him. I engaged a firm of private detectives to make inquiries.'

'We agreed to take up the case,' put in Mrs. Destry, speaking for the first time since she had arrived. 'That was my husband's business, and I assisted him. Actually, my husband had retired, but he was always willing to take on a case if the person concerned was recommended by an old client. Miss Marsh was, and when he heard her story he was very interested. By a curious coincidence, we were living at Evesham Mansions; we were tenants there before Sir Franklin bought the property. We made very little headway until The Yellow Orchid was opened. We had only one clue to work on regarding the identity of this man we were trying to find for Miss Marsh.'

'My father noticed it once during one

of the interviews he had,' said Audrey. 'It was a windy night, and the wind shook one of the shutters, moving it sufficiently to let in a ray of moonlight. It was only for an instant, just a momentary gleam, and it fell on the man's hand.'

'The Intaglio ring!' broke in Gordan.

She nodded.

'Then that's what Myra Destry meant in the notebook,' exclaimed Gordan. 'That's what she managed to say just before she died.'

'Who *was* Myra Destry?' inquired Mr. Budd.

'She was my husband's sister,' answered Mrs. Destry. 'She'd helped Richard before, and when we heard from Miss Marsh that her father had been given instructions to open The Yellow Orchid, we thought she might be useful. She was an attractive woman. We thought if she became a *habitué* of the place, she might learn something.'

'She did,' said Gordan a little grimly.

'Yes,' said Mrs. Destry. 'On the night she was murdered, I think she was very near the truth.'

'Why did she call herself Myra?' asked

the reporter. 'That's your name, isn't it? Surely it wasn't — '

'No, her name was Sonia,' said Mrs. Destry. 'It was Richard's idea that she should use my name.'

'Why?' murmured Mr. Budd.

'So that any message that Williams had for her could legitimately be addressed to Evesham Mansions.'

'Williams!' exclaimed Gordan. 'Do you mean *Nosey* Williams?'

'Yes,' said Mrs. Destry. 'He was getting us information, any odd scraps that he could pick up. He worked for my husband in the old days, and when Miss Marsh gave us this job, he contacted Williams again as the person most likely to help.'

'I see,' said Gordan. 'No wonder Nosey didn't want to part with any information to me. You were paying him better, I suppose?'

'We were paying him very well,' said Mrs. Destry. 'I think he got frightened after Sonia was killed. It was very difficult to get anything out of him after that.'

'I s'pose it was from Williams that you

learned that this feller you was after was Mr. Midnight?' grunted Mr. Budd.

Mrs. Destry nodded. 'Yes,' she answered.

'Did he tell you who Midnight is?'

It was Audrey who replied. 'Yes. I wanted to see this thing through on my own, but now you've arrested my father, I've *got* to tell you.'

'Who *is* Midnight?' asked Gordan eagerly.

'Rodney Mayne,' she said.

Gordan Cross looked at her, his astonishment rendering him incapable of speech for the moment. Mr. Budd showed neither surprise nor any other emotion. His face wore its usual expression of sleepy boredom.

'Rodney Mayne,' repeated Gordan, expelling his breath. 'So *he's* at the bottom of all this.'

'Yes,' Audrey answered. 'Rodney Mayne is responsible for everything.'

''Ave you got proof of that, miss?' inquired Mr. Budd.

'You'll find all the proof you require at his flat.'

'Well, well,' murmured Mr. Budd, shaking his head. 'Who'd have believed that a nice young feller like that could be a cold-blooded murderer and the brains behind a racket like this Midnight business. Hm . . . it just shows you never can tell. An' he is the feller who been blackmailin' your father?'

'Yes, of course,' she said.

'He killed Richard because he knew we'd found out about him,' said Mrs. Destry. 'He would have killed me too, if he could have got hold of me; only Miss Marsh insisted on my going down to her cottage in the country.'

'You must do something at once,' broke in Audrey. 'While Mayne's at large, Mrs. Destry's in danger.'

'Now don't you worry,' said Mr. Budd soothingly. 'Nothin's going to 'appen to Mrs. Destry — not now. I'll deal with Mayne.'

'I suppose he's at The Yellow Orchid now,' said Gordan, glancing at the clock.

'Oh no he ain't,' said Mr. Budd. 'There's no one at The Yellow Orchid. The Yellow Orchid's closed.'

'Supposing he gets suspicious and tries to make a getaway?' said Gordan.

'He won't,' said the big man placidly. 'Don't you go gettin' excited. I've got this all worked out.'

'You're not trying to tell me that you knew it was Mayne all along,' said the reporter.

Mr. Budd shook his head. 'No, because I didn't,' he replied.

'You don't seem very surprised.'

'I can't say I am, Mr. Cross. You see, it 'ad to be someone.'

'Well, that's obvious. But I never expected it would turn out to be Mayne.'

'I ought to 'ave guessed who it 'ud be,' said Mr. Budd. 'Mayne was the most likely chap, when you come to think of it.''

Mrs. Destry looked surprised. 'I must say that it was quite a shock to me,' she said.

Mr. Budd looked at her and slowly shook his head. 'That's because you don't understand. I don't think I've ever come across a similar sort o' case in all my experience.'

'What's so extraordinary about it?' asked Gordan.

'The thing that's so extraordinary is

that it's so very ordinary. All simple an' straightforward — except for the trimmin's.' He was interrupted by the sound of a knock on the front door.

'Who's that?' said Gordan.

'Brill 'ull answer it,' said Mr. Budd, but his sleepy eyes were suddenly alert. 'I think it's the person we want make the whole thing complete.'

Gordan heard Brill's heavy tread go along the passage, and the door opened. There was the muttering of voices, and after a moment, Leek came in. 'I've brought him,' he announced.

'Good!' said Mr. Budd. He got ponderously to his feet. 'Bring him in, will you?'

The lean sergeant nodded and went out.

'Who is it?' asked Gordan.

'Somebody you'll like to meet, Mr. Cross,' said Mr. Budd. 'Somebody you've been wantin' to meet for a long time. Mr. Midnight.'

'Mayne — ' began the reporter.

'Oh, no,' said Mr. Budd gently. 'Mayne isn't Mr. Midnight. *This* is Mr. Midnight.'

Leek and Brill came into the room on either side of Franklin Marsh.

22

'It was a very clever idea when you come to work it out,' remarked Mr. Budd later the same evening, as he sat drinking coffee in Gordan Cross's flat. 'Foresight, I s'pose you'd call it.'

'I don't quite understand it all yet,' confessed Vicky, back once again in her own home and looking none worse for her brief sojourn at the police station. 'Do you mean that all this business about Sir Franklin being blackmailed, and his daughter engaging the Destrys to find out who was blackmailing him, was a fake?'

'That's it, Mrs. Cross,' said the superintendent, nodding. 'You might call it an elaborately prepared alibi in case anything went wrong.'

'Then Audrey Marsh was in it, too?'

'Oh yes, she was in it up to her neck. She'll be charged as an accessory with her father.' He gulped down the remainder of his coffee. 'You see,' he went on, 'when Sir Franklin Marsh started this Midnight racket, he realized that sooner or later someone 'ud begin to wonder where 'e was gettin' all his money from. From bein' dead broke, he suddenly blossomed into a very rich man, buyin' property all over the place. It was only natural that the police would be gettin' suspicious and want to know where it all came from. So 'e an' 'is daughter concocted this entire scheme.

'They hatched a totally mythical story about a mysterious man who was blackmailin' Sir Franklin because of some equally mythical thing 'e'd done against the law, an' they engaged Destry an' 'is wife to try an' find 'im. To make the whole thing look more authentic, Audrey Marsh adopted the name of Audrey Smith an' flitted around like one of those mysterious figures in a crime story. Sir Franklin introduced the clue of the Intaglio ring — another bit out of a thriller — an' the whole stage was set. They selected Rodney Mayne for the scapegoat an' began to scatter clues around that 'ud lead the Destrys to him.

'Unfortunately, 'owever, Sonia — or, as she called herself, Myra — began to cotton on to the same situation an' had to be got rid of. They were afraid that she had told somethin' to Laddie Castell, an' so that bomb was planned at the empty house at Barnet. When that didn't come off, Castell was killed another way. They searched 'is flat in case there was anything that Sonia had written to 'im, or left with 'im, an' that note from 'A. Smith' was left for you, just to make everythin' look genuine.'

'Was it Marsh who killed Sonia Destry and Castell?' asked Vicky.

'It was,' said Mr. Budd, 'an' Nosey Williams an' Richard Destry.'

'Why did he kill Destry?' asked Gordan.

'Because Destry found out that the whole idea of the mysterious blackmailer was a fake. You and Mrs. Cross would have been killed too, if you'd been gettin' dangerous. Sir Franklin was quite ruthless, an' he hoped that Mayne would suffer for anything he did.'

'The Destrys were quite genuine,

then?' said Vicky.

'Oh, yes. They *had* to be, you see,' said Mr. Budd. 'Their evidence was essential when the balloon went up an' Sir Franklin Marsh had to be exonerated an' sympathized with as the unfortunate victim of a blackmailin' scoundrel. It was all very cleverly worked out — Mayne the scapegoat and Sir Franklin Marsh virtually givin' up the property had been forced to buy — except, of course, a few 'undred thousand that 'ad been salted away an' nobody knew anythin' about.'

He held out his cup and Vicky poured out some more coffee.

'Well, it's all over now. These things never work out, you know, though criminals are always 'opin' they will. You'd think they'd get wise the fact after all the examples they've 'ad, but they never will. They always think that *they're* the ones that are goin' to be too clever. Vanity — that's what it is.'

He pulled out one of his black cigars and looked at appreciatively.

'You're not going to smoke that in here,' said Vicky decidedly. 'I'm willing to put up with a lot of things, but there *are* limits.'

Mr. Budd sighed. Reluctantly, he put the cigar away.

THE FACELESS ONES
GRIM DEATH
MURDER IN MANUSCRIPT
THE GLASS ARROW
THE THIRD KEY
THE ROYAL FLUSH MURDERS
THE SQUEALER
MR. WHIPPLE EXPLAINS
THE SEVEN CLUES
THE CHAINED MAN
THE HOUSE OF THE GOAT
THE FOOTBALL POOL MURDERS
THE HAND OF FEAR
SORCERER'S HOUSE
THE HANGMAN
THE CON MAN
MISTER BIG
THE JOCKEY
THE SILVER HORSESHOE
THE TUDOR GARDEN MYSTERY
THE SHOW MUST GO ON
SINISTER HOUSE
THE WITCHES' MOON
ALIAS THE GHOST
THE LADY OF DOOM

THE BLACK HUNCHBACK
PHANTOM HOLLOW
WHITE WIG
THE GHOST SQUAD
THE NEXT TO DIE
THE WHISPERING WOMAN
THE TWELVE APOSTLES
THE GRIM JOKER
THE HUNTSMAN
THE NIGHTMARE MURDERS
THE TIPSTER
THE VAMPIRE MAN
THE RED TAPE MURDERS
THE FRIGHTENED MAN
THE TOKEN

With Chris Verner:
THE BIG FELLOW
THE SNARK WAS A BOOJUM

WRAITH OF VENGEANCE

Edmund Glasby

Contemplating a scheme to plunder a sinister Venetian island of a rumoured hoard, a tour company advisor finds more there than he bargained for . . . The group gathered for the reading of a will get the shock of their lives . . . A distant oil-drilling platform endures a bizarre siege . . . A man undergoes a hideous transformation . . . The night shift in a morgue takes a deadly turn . . . In an English village on All Hallows Eve, an ancient evil reawakens. Six tales of horror and the macabre by Edmund Glasby.

SILENCE OF THE BONES

Arlette Lees

Rodeo star Coby Dillon vanishes in a storm on the very evening he was to set up house with his girlfriend Brielle Broussard. Where is he — and what has become of his mentor Dyce Dean Jackson? Meanwhile, Deputy Sheriffs Robely Danner and Frack Tilsley — partners in both work and love — are investigating reports of poisonous contaminated moonshine. And Robely's mother Gladys Calhoun is brutally attacked in the night. All these seemingly disparate events are connected by a thread of blood . . .